JONAH

JONAH

RED RAIN #7

RACHEL NEWHOUSE

rachelnewhouse.com

To Dustin
For being the perfect reader

To Kris
For being the kind of wife and mother
I want to be when I grow up

JULY 2076

1: NIC

I should have known my ex-girlfriend would try to kill me.

To her credit, she'd set the stage beautifully. She'd trapped us on the Bridge of Seventeen Arches, where the moonlit water prevented any heroic escape. A pair of guards stood behind her on the west bank, while another set approached from across the bridge. On the other side of the lake, Beijing's iconic Summer Palace sprawled on the hill, aglow with the light and music of the annual United state dinner. It was a stunning backdrop for a crime of passion.

She slithered towards us, the clack of her stilettos on the brick more irritating than threatening. "Dr. Von Nieuwenhuyse, you're under arrest."

I took a step back, mostly to avoid her overpowering perfume. "You've been saving up for that one, haven't you, Asia?"

She flicked her tongue like she had hair in her mouth. "You can call me Min," she said, referring to one of three of her given names.

"I could call you a lot of things, but there are children present," I returned. I shoved Philadelphia, my ward, behind me, even though I knew it was a wasted gesture.

Phil glanced rapidly between us, as if the motion could help her sheltered seventeen-year-old brain catch up. "Are you two—"

I put my hand up. "*Were.* Whatever you were about to say, it's past tense."

"Nic," Asia scolded, "you didn't even give me a chance."

"If you wanted a chance, you shouldn't have led with 'you're under arrest.' I have standards."

"I got desperate," Asia said in a tone that suggested she was anything but.

"I just never pictured you as someone who would be in a relationship. Ever," Phil commented, eyeing me like this revelation changed everything.

"And you wonder why." I gestured at Asia.

She took it as a compliment. "We have so much to catch up on. I've been waiting eight years for you to accept my invitation." She beckoned to her guards, who advanced like a noose cinching.

I stuck both of my arms out to stop them. "Hold on, let's get one thing straight. I'm Andromeda's plus one, *not* yours," I said, using Phil's legal name.

"Wait, you've been waiting *eight years*?" Phil shoved my arm aside and faced Asia. "Why didn't you just arrest him while he was on Mars?"

"An excellent observation," I praised. I folded my arms and glared at Asia. "If you're so madly in love with me, why didn't you propose before now? You knew exactly where I was."

I remembered, despite my best attempts, the day we broke up. Asia had been just as wealthy and powerful then as she was now; she could have easily had me arrested, or defunded my science station on Mars, or employed any number of threatening tactics. But she hadn't. She'd accepted her defeat and slunk into the shadows, and the only contact I received from her was an annual invitation to the state gala. It wasn't until recently that I realized she'd even been paying attention to what I was experimenting with on Mars.

Asia stroked one of the marble dragons that capped the bridge's railing. "You don't think this is the perfect place to get engaged?"

"As much as I appreciate the effort that went into this elaborate set-up, no, this seems ill thought out." It made no sense for Asia to wait so long, only to confront me in a public place. Even though there was no one else on the bridge, there were still people nearby. People that might ask questions—or worse, tell Asia's father.

General Secretary Mong, the supreme leader of the United, had not been privy to my romance with Asia—or the various illegal schemes she and I had attempted together. I'm sure he'd be fascinated to know that his own daughter had helped me create a world-ending superweapon designed to bring his empire to its knees.

No, nothing about this macabre play made sense for Asia, and that was what I found most threatening.

"Why now, Asia?" I demanded.

She giggled, a disgusting little sound. "Isn't it obvious?"

"No," I admitted, knowing full well I was about to lose.

Asia strolled over and grabbed Phil's arm. I reacted, but the guards were faster. I heard the distinct sound of an electric gun powering up and froze.

And that's when I remembered I was also carrying.

Asia pulled Phil towards her. Phil stopped breathing, her panicked blue eyes begging me to help. I could only watch as Asia ran her deadly manicured nails through Philadelphia's ashy blonde curls.

"It's been so long since the great Dr. Von Nieuwenhuyse has cared about anyone but himself..." Asia cooed. She hooked one finger under the pearl necklace Philadelphia wore—the necklace I had given Asia as a gift so many years ago. Asia yanked on the chain, and Phil gasped, clutching her throat.

Asia held her there and looked up at me, bloodred lips curled in a sneer. "I simply couldn't waste the opportunity."

Suddenly, Asia's eight years of silence made sense. Philadelphia changed everything, as she had an annoying habit of doing. Three months ago, Phil had been my enemy, an incessant reminder of my failure. But somewhere in the process of escaping from prison, destroying my own superweapon, and generally doing our best to get ourselves killed, we'd mutually agreed to update our status. I'd signed a paper making her my legal dependent, and that paper gave Asia the card she needed to play her hand.

For the first time in years, I was a man with something to lose.

"You're right," I admitted. "That should have been obvious."

Asia let Phil go, and she jerked away. "You've been using me?" she screeched at Asia.

"Catch up, darling," I admonished. "It's basic blackmail."

"Was this your plan the whole time?" Phil demanded.

"If you mean to imply that I orchestrated this whole 'thunderbird' revolution as bait to lure Nic back to Earth..." Asia flicked her fingers, as if the resistance movement was no more inconvenient than a crumb to be brushed off the table. "Then no. I had nothing to do with your adorable little videos trending. I just know an opportunity when I see one."

Phil slid behind me, even though she probably would have been safer literally anywhere else. "You're disgusting."

"Now you know why we broke up." I took a rallying breath. "Any other clarifying questions? Because we should probably speed this up. That party isn't going to last forever, and eventually other people are going to want to use this bridge for something other than a standoff."

"I'm ready to go if you are. Shall we?" Asia nodded at the west bank, where her guards waited.

I took a step towards her. Phil grabbed my arm. "Nic, you can't!"

"Honey, were you not listening to her evil monologue?" I grabbed Phil's wrist and pried her hand off my jacket. "If I don't do as she says, she'll kill you or something equally pedantic."

Asia cackled. "I usually warm up with some light torture. Give me some credit."

"Well, today's your lucky day, because I don't feel like listening to Andi scream. It's a horribly irritating sound, and I already have a headache." I strode up to Asia, folded one hand behind my back, and bowed. "Shall we go get a coffee? I'll buy."

She jerked back. "Beg pardon?"

"I said, let's go get coffee. Hang on, let me make sure I brought my phone so I can pay." I patted my pockets. As I did so, I subtly pressed the button on the pistol I had holstered under my jacket.

I grunted to cover the whir of it powering on. "Okay, good to go. You, me, date." I looked back up at Asia and held out my hand.

She eyed it like a dead fish.

"That's what you want, isn't it? Us, together. If I go with you, there's no reason Andi can't go home, right? Or did I miss something?"

"There' are a couple of other things I want, but..." Asia grasped my hand and pulled me towards her. "This is a good place to start, if you're offering."

Phil finally found her voice. "Nic, don't—"

"Shh," I hissed over my shoulder, "the adults are talking."

I leaned into Asia, pushing her against the railing. Her guards shifted, but Asia put her hand up. "I can handle this one," she crooned, her dark eyes mocking me.

I put my lips close to hers, then stopped. I watched out of my peripheral until I saw one of the guards power off his weapon and slide it into his holster.

"Min," I whispered quietly enough that only she could hear. "There's something I should tell you."

"Yes?" she begged.

I took a deep breath. "I'm *not* sorry it had to be this way."

And then I grasped her shoulders and shoved her over the railing.

She tumbled into the water with a shriek and a very satisfying splash. The guards on the bank reacted immediately, diving into the lake after her.

The two on the bridge were slower on the draw. "Aren't you going to rescue your boss?" I taunted.

They fumbled with their weapons.

"No? Then you're fired." I whipped my warmed-up pistol out of my jacket and shot them both.

Phil screamed. So much for avoiding that ear-splitting sound.

"Run!" I shouted unnecessarily. She kicked off her shoes and raced after me, abandoning her heels in the middle of the bridge like Cinderella.

Asia got her head above water long enough to shout something wholly inappropriate after us.

It was a stupidly long bridge, and I cursed every one of its ostentatious arches as we passed. At this rate, they'd have Asia fished out of the water before we got to the other side.

A few guards were posted on the east bank, checking invitations like some imperial bouncers. They rushed to meet us at the foot of the bridge, no doubt drawn by the distant sound of Asia's enraged yelling.

"There's been a fight!" I exclaimed before they could ask. "Some lady fell in the water—you have to help her!"

The promise of a damsel in distress did the trick. The guards raced onto the bridge, shouting orders at each other. Attempting to look casual, I hooked my arm with Phil's and hurried her across the courtyard to the street, where a throng of enterprising cab drivers waited to feast on drunk party guests.

One hapless lad ran ahead of the others and got to me first. "Do you need a ride, sir?" he begged in broken English.

"More than you know." I gestured for him to lead the way.

He darted to his car on the curb and opened the door. I waited until he had helped Phil into the back seat, then pulled my gun on him.

"Keys," I demanded.

The driver barked his disagreement in Mandarin, so I turned and shot the person standing closest to us to reinforce my point.

"Nic!" Phil screamed, and several other passersby joined her.

The driver wisely decided the vehicle wasn't worth his life. He threw his keyring at me, shouting about how he was going to report this.

"Asia's way ahead of you," I droned, and shot him to end the conversation.

The crowd devolved into a panic as everyone graciously got out of my way. I ran to the driver's door and jumped in. I jammed the key in the ignition and swiped commands onto the car's overly complicated control panel. Thankfully, it was a cheap vehicle and didn't have any inconvenient safety features like face recognition, so it started on the first turn. I slammed on the gas, clipping the rear of the car ahead of me as I jerked away from the curb.

Phil squealed in tune to the crunching metal. "Nic, what are you doing?"

"Don't worry, it was set on stun." I navigated out of the parking lot, slowing down just long enough to make an inconspicuous turn into traffic. I waited until we were a few blocks away before checking the mirrors; there were no flashing lights in my peripheral.

I sped up as much as I could without drawing attention to ourselves. "Turn off your phone," I barked at Phil.

"J-Jayde has my phone," she returned, voice warbly from adrenaline.

I shot her an incredulous glance in the rearview mirror. She shrugged. "This dress doesn't have pockets."

"Well, I guess that will give them a beacon to find his body." We'd left Jayde back at the palace, lying unconscious on the third-floor balcony of the Tower of Incense. He was Phil's former ally in the underground—strong emphasis on *former*. He had blackmailed Phil into going to this cursed party as part of an absurd assassination plot. I could only hope the government would find him and make him regret his life choices.

Keeping one eye on the crowded road, I fished my phone out of my pocket and turned it off. "Asia will have our files flagged as soon as she gets dried off. If we stay offline, it will buy us some time."

I glared at the darkened screen of my device as my own words sank into me. I'd never been friends with the law, but I'd always had my clean identity—and my secluded science station on Mars—to fall back on. At any point, I could have shut up, minded my own business, and lived happily ever after in my castle in the stars.

Not anymore. With a few keystrokes, Asia would turn me and Andromeda Nolan—Philadelphia's legal identity—into the United's most wanted criminals. We wouldn't be able to even check our email without alerting the authorities, much less buy a transit ticket off the planet.

"So much for going back to Mars," I grunted, hurling my phone onto the passenger seat.

Phil said nothing. As much as silence was my preferred mode of conversation, I was smart enough to know that no reaction to circumstances as dire as ours was a bad sign. I looked at her in the rearview mirror and saw all the telltale signs of a panic attack. Her whole body was rigid as she gripped the door handle. She stared out the window with glassy eyes, her shoulders heaving with shallow breaths.

"You need to breathe slowly," I commanded. "Try to lower your heart rate by at least fifty beats per minute."

She glared at me. "Is that your way of telling me to calm down?"

I shrugged. "I figured the specific directions were more helpful."

She grimaced. With great effort, she pried her hand off the door handle and clenched it in her lap. "I don't... know if I can calm down," she admitted.

"Keep practicing," I deadpanned. "You're going to need the calories."

She frowned.

I turned my attention back to the road. "We're going to be running for a very long time."

2: PHILADELPHIA

So much for going back to Mars.

I struggled to obey Nic's instructions, but the more I tried to breathe slowly, the more I felt my throat cinching shut. I was painfully aware of my pulse as my heart slammed into my ribs. My head was buzzing, and the only thing I could hear were the echoes of a hundred accusations.

This was all my fault, again. I'd known for a while that I could never go back to a quiet life on Mars; I'd made that choice when I accepted the title of "Blue Fire." I thought I could lead a revolution—I thought *God* wanted me to lead a revolution.

But I was an idiot. I made a mistake by going to Beijing, and now everything was ruined. My file was marked, the revolution was in shambles, and Jayde had tried to kill me.

Nic had saved me from getting thrown off a balcony, but now he was stuck on Earth with me. I had made us both criminals, and if the United investigated Nic's file, the base on Mars would be the next to fall. What would happen to my brother Ephesus and Nic's sister, Cea? Ephesus had just gotten back to Mars, and he was an accomplice in as many crimes as I was. The government wouldn't hesitate to arrest him—or worse—when they found out where he was hiding. And what of the base's other residents, like the Sardises? They had been nothing but kind to me, and now I was putting them all in danger.

All because I didn't listen to Nic when he told me to come home.

You are not a hero, Andromeda.

"We need a place to go," Nic interrupted my inner monologue. "At least to get some supplies and a change of clothes. You won't last twenty-four hours on the street in that dress."

I looked down at the crumpled layers of silk around my waist. He was right, and he would fare only marginally better in his white suit jacket and slick pants.

Unfortunately, I'd only been in Beijing for four days and didn't know anything about the city. We couldn't go back to my house. The Nolans, my adopted family, had a gorgeous estate with everything we could possibly need, but Asia would have it locked down within the hour. There was only one other person in this entire country that I knew by name, and there was no guarantee she'd be at her studio.

"Narissa," I offered. "My stylist."

Nic arched an eyebrow. "Do you trust her? She worked for Thames."

"I do," I said, and then tried to quantify why. "She knew what I was planning on doing."

I rubbed my right palm and felt the tiny computer chip that was buried just beneath my skin. Even though I couldn't see it, I knew there was a network of wires woven through my fingers that turned my palm into a weapon. If I had shaken the Secretary General's hand back at the party, the computer in my skin would have reacted to his DNA and sent him into cardiac arrest with an electromagnetic shock. It would have been the perfect assassination.

And I almost went through with it.

I resisted the urge to crush the chip. The last thing I needed was for the wiring to short circuit and electrocute me.

"Narissa knew what was going on," I said, forcing my attention back to the present. "She didn't have all the details, but she knew Jayde and I were planning something and wanted to help. She made the dress." I fingered the jagged silver embroidery that decorated my skirt like lightning, turning me into a living thunderbird.

"I don't see what a costume change has to do with it," Nic commented, "but hopefully she still likes you more than the United."

I swallowed. Narissa's motivations were a mystery to me, but she'd been willing to die to help me become Blue Fire. Hopefully, that generosity would extend a little further—if she was even home.

I gave Nic the name of Narissa's studio, and he keyed it into the cab's navigation system. Thankfully, it was only fifteen minutes away.

"We're going to have to ditch the car a few blocks away and walk in," Nic said as he turned into an abandoned alley. The vehicle pitched as we rolled over water-filled potholes. "As soon as the driver wakes up and turns in a report, they'll start tracking the cab."

Nic parked behind an apartment building with a cluster of other sketchy cars. I opened the cab door and instantly remembered I was barefoot. I gingerly stepped onto the cold concrete, swallowing a wince. Now that the adrenaline was wearing off, my bloody heels were screaming in agony.

Nic had the grace to slow down and wait for me as I picked my way around trash and sharp pieces of gravel. We skirted the backs of buildings until we came to Narissa's shop. The alley lights were not on; I prayed that meant we couldn't be easily seen on any security cameras.

"What's your plan if she's not home?" Nic asked as we climbed the steps to the rear door.

"Pray and ask God for a brilliant idea," I replied.

He snorted. I didn't bother to tell him that was my actual plan.

Thankfully, Plan B wasn't necessary. I rapped on the door with my knuckles, and it opened instantly.

Narissa stood there. She took in my scuffed heels and muddy hem with her sharp eyes. "I thought you said you weren't going to be running."

"There was a change of plans," I confessed.

"I know, I saw the news." She held the door open and waved us inside.

Mercifully, her shop was deserted. The shades were drawn, and all the lights were dark. The waterfall that decorated the rear wall was off, a few drips of water still glinting on the glass. "I'm surprised you're still at work," I commented.

She locked the door behind us. "I wasn't. But when I saw that your appearance at the party was surprisingly uneventful, I figured something had gone wrong, and you might need me."

I took in her appearance. This was the most casual I'd ever seen her; she had no makeup on, and she wore loose sweats that seemed completely out of character. "Thank you for coming back," I said, and directed the same at Jesus.

She turned to Nic and offered her hand. "I assume you're the wild card of the night. Q, is it? Pleased to finally make your acquaintance."

After a flicker of hesitation, he accepted the handshake. "Just Nic, please."

She snorted. "You'd better get used to the nickname, Q. Sounds like you two will be going back to codenames for a while. This way." She flicked her fingers and led us towards the elevator.

We descended two floors beneath the building to Narissa's private studio. I let her get off the elevator first, then grabbed Nic's sleeve to hold him back. "Be careful what you say around her," I hissed.

"I thought you said you trusted her!" he snapped, shrugging me off.

"I do, but she's got eye implants. The algorithm hears everything." I remembered when Narissa had taken out her contacts and shown her robotic eyes to me. The implants had cured her of blindness, and she could take measurements, manipulate dress patterns, and match the perfect foundation shade, all just by thinking about it. But in exchange, the government saw everything she saw and heard everything she heard—the perfect form of control.

Nic muttered something foul. "Well, hopefully the government hasn't updated its search parameters yet," he grunted and stepped off the elevator.

Narissa clapped her hands. The lights in the studio flickered on, revealing the futuristic dress fabricator that dominated the floor. Its robotic needles were frozen in mid-air, the unfinished form of a bodice abandoned on the cutting board.

I walked up and looked inside the glass at the sleek black garment. The material was stiff but had an otherworldly sheen to it, like it was a cross between leather and silk. Complex embroidery flared from the neckline; the layered stitching made the sleeve look like it was made of feathers.

"The design's not finished. I need to start over." Narissa grasped my shoulders and steered me away. "There are men's clothes in the closet over there—take what you need. I can fit them if necessary," she said to Nic. "You, on the other hand, should be glad you left your change of clothes here this morning. I don't carry many practical women's outfits." She grabbed a pile of clothes off a drafting table and pushed me into a fitting room, shutting the door behind us.

I obediently turned around and let her unzip my dress. "Thank you for helping us."

"I don't want to know the details. Just tell me one thing." She paused, her eyes finding mine in the mirror. "Did something go wrong, or did you change your mind?"

I swallowed. "I changed my mind." *Too little too late.*

She grunted and helped me step out of the dress. "Well, at least you made a good impression on Mong."

She wasn't wrong. Instead of shaking the General's hand, I'd bowed. He'd been pleased with my show of humility and had taken a shining to me, although I think that had more to do with the Holy Spirit than any charisma of mine. I'd even invited him over for dinner—and he'd accepted.

Not that the social capital would do me any good after Asia flagged my file.

"What are you going to do with the dress?" I asked.

Narissa held the cloud of gray-blue silk up to the light and examined a seam. "I'll wash and mend it. You're going to need it again."

It was said with finality, so I didn't argue, even though I highly doubted I'd have an occasion to dress up for a ball again. My days as an elite Nolan were over.

I grabbed the stack of clothes off the stool. It was the outfit I'd changed out of this morning, along with my little black backpack. My heart lurched at the sight of it. There was nothing of monetary value in there, but at least I would have the leather-bound Bible my boyfriend Stanyard had given me.

I shivered as I quickly changed into my ripped jeans, nondescript t-shirt, and black leather jacket. What would Stanyard say when he found out what happened? Jayde had threatened to kill him if I didn't go to Beijing and complete the assassination, which we'd codenamed "Operation Thunderbird." Nic said he'd taken care of it and gotten Stanyard to safety. I believed him, but that didn't change the fact that I'd lied to my best friend.

The last time I'd seen Stanyard, he'd convinced me not to go along with the operation. He'd also told me he loved me—and instead of saying "I love you, too" like a normal person, I'd kissed him.

Then, not six hours later, I'd dropped off the grid and boarded a flight to Beijing, apparently going back on everything I'd just said. What must he think of me? I knew Stanyard well enough to trust that he'd forgive me in time. But what would he say when he found out I'd almost started a war and sacrificed millions of people just to save him?

My dad had done the same thing when he created Red Rain, Nic's chemical superweapon. He'd given the government the keys to the apocalypse in exchange for my life. When I'd learned the truth, I'd felt enraged, betrayed, and abandoned.

I had no doubts Stanyard would feel the same.

I shrugged the backpack on, feeling the weight settle between my shoulders along with the heaviness in my heart. *Jesus, I'm so sorry. I should have trusted You.*

Narissa opened the fitting room door. I quickly pulled on my boots and walked back out into the studio. Nic, in typical male fashion, had clearly gotten dressed in thirty seconds and spent the rest of the time pacing the room. He now wore jeans, a plain button-up, and a light windbreaker. I missed his perpetual lab coat already, although I would never have admitted that to him.

"I need to get online before they flag my file," he declared as soon as we came out of the fitting room.

Narissa gestured at a laptop that was precariously balanced on a stack of fabric bolts. Nic took it, sat down cross-legged on the floor, and started typing rapidly.

"Me too. I need to send a message to Stanyard. Is it safe to text him?" I looked to Nic for permission. The last thing I wanted to do was get someone killed because I spoke too soon.

"You can text whoever you want before they flag your file," he said, clearly not listening to me. He pulled his phone out of his pocket, powered it on, and tossed it at me.

I caught it gracelessly. I opened the encrypted messaging app and saw that Stanyard—or "Aurelius," as he went by online— was a pinned contact. He was not online.

I started a new chat and hesitated with my thumbs over the screen. How could I cram a heartfelt apology and an explanation of a near-death experience into one message?

"Just tell him you're going offline so he doesn't worry," Nic offered, apparently noticing the fact that my fingers weren't moving.

I chewed my lip and tried to follow his advice.

HEY. IT'S BLUE FIRE. I'M SAFE, Q'S WITH ME. WE HAVE TO GO OFFLINE FOR A WHILE. I WILL CALL WHEN I CAN. I LOVE YOU.

I hit send, then added:

I'M SO SORRY

3: NIC

I watched out of the corner of my eye as Phil stood there, staring dumbly at the phone in her hand. No doubt she was hoping Pizza Boy would come online and call her. When he didn't, she handed the device back to me with a sigh.

I took it and leaned it against the laptop's screen to pair the devices. "You need to wash your makeup off. Your eyeliner is running."

She glared at me, but there was nothing to be offended about. It was a factual statement.

"There's makeup wipes in the bathroom. Here, let me take your extension out." Narissa held Phil still with one hand and used the other to remove a clip of fake curls from her hair. Phil's bleached locks fell to her shoulders, tired and stringy—not unlike the girl they were attached to.

Narissa herded her into the bathroom and shut the door after her. I turned my attention back to the laptop. I'd remotely logged into my private server on Mars. I tabbed through the database and started downloading as many files as I could to my phone. Contacts, music, blackmail—anything I might need while we were on the move for the next several weeks.

Narissa approached me. "Where are you going to go?"

"I know some safe houses," I lied. The truth was that both of my safe havens—the base on Mars and my parents' house—would become death traps once Asia staked them out. But anywhere would be preferable to Beijing, and if I could get out of the city and call Ephesus on a secured line, we could figure something out.

Probably.

Narissa wisely didn't ask for more details. She grabbed a backpack off the floor and dumped the contents onto a cutting table. "I don't have much by way of survival supplies here, but what I have you're welcome to." She walked over to her mini fridge and started stuffing water bottles and snacks into the bag.

"Thank you," I said with as much sincerity as I knew how to convey. My phone screeched at me, complaining about its storage being full. I cancelled the remaining downloads with a grunt. "I'd recommend copying what you need off this laptop and doing a factory reset. Then they won't be able to catch you with any incriminating files. Some of the info I downloaded isn't exactly legal."

"Keep the laptop." She yanked a bolt of wool out of the middle of a stack of fabric, causing the rest of the bolts to tumble onto the floor. "Just reregister it under your name—please."

I nodded and navigated to the settings. "What's your plan when Asia shows up? They'll know I accessed your Wi-Fi."

"Don't worry about me." She threw the wool on the cutting board and measured out a generous portion. "I've got as much dirt on Asia as she has on me. We're in this together. Besides, she knows you trust me. She's better off leaving me alone and hoping you'll come back, looking for help." She slid her scissors down the groove in the cutting board with deadly swiftness. "So don't come back."

"Wasn't planning on it." I hesitated on the laptop's registration page, debating. Then, with a couple of clicks, I changed the ownership to Andromeda.

Narissa dropped the backpack on the floor next to me. "I wasn't worried about you."

Just then, Phil came out of the bathroom. With her makeup gone and her hair down, she'd transformed from a manicured princess back into a sullen teenager. Her eyes were swollen and bloodshot, and I could tell the night was catching up to her. We'd be lucky if we made it three blocks before she collapsed, which meant we needed to get moving.

I powered off my devices and stuffed them in the backpack. "Any recommendations for someone who can get us out of the country?" I asked Narissa.

She rolled up the makeshift blanket and helped me strap it to the backpack. "You don't need to get out of the country. You need to get off the grid."

I didn't disagree, but that was a tall order in the world's most heavily surveilled and technologically advanced country. "Any recommendations?" I countered.

I wasn't expecting an answer, but to my surprise, Narissa had one. "Jael."

I looked up at her. "Who?"

Narissa put her palms forward. "I haven't met her, but I've heard of her. They say she's got connections in the tech world and can get anyone off the grid."

"That sounds too good to be true," I intoned.

Narissa shrugged. "She once hid an entire church congregation and broke the pastor out of jail hours before his execution—all without leaving a trace. They say she hacked into the police chief's cell phone and even remotely edited the security footage."

That sounded like a straight-up fairytale, but the notion of Christians getting romantically rescued from death was enough to convince Phil that this mystical woman was our savior. "Where can we find her?" she said, eyes wide with gullible wonder.

"Even if I knew where she was, I wouldn't tell you." Narissa tapped her temple, reminding us all of her implants. "But you don't just *find* Jael. You have to find someone who knows her, and they'll take you to her."

I stood up and shouldered the backpack. "And where, exactly, do these followers of Jael like to congregate?"

Narissa must not have liked my tone of voice, because she gave me a frown that could have curdled butter. "Your best bet is to find someone who attends *jiating jiaohui.*"

"What?" Phil asked.

"House church," I answered, and then regretted it when Narissa whipped her head to stare at me. She arched an eyebrow, the thin line of plucked hairs curling like a cat's tail.

In her defense, I probably shouldn't have known what that phrase meant. But being a highly educated individual—and hanging out with elites like Asia—had taught me some functional Mandarin, and I was more versed in religious terminology than I cared to admit. But the fact that I had personal experience with the Chinese Christian community was not information Phil needed to have right now, so I kept the conversation moving.

"That will be easier said than done," I muttered. "It's an underground church for a reason."

Associating with anything but the Chinese state religion had been risky fifty years ago. Now even the state religion was illegal, and claiming to be Protestant was a swift way to meet Jesus.

None of this deterred Phil. "Any idea where to look? Surely you know someone."

Narissa opened her mouth, but the trill of an alarm spared her the trouble. "That would be Asia." She strode over to a computer terminal and brought up a security feed. Sure enough, Asia and half a dozen guards stood outside, pounding on the front door.

I cursed. I knew our luck was too good to last.

"She was quick." Narissa squinted at the screen. "Why is her hair wet? She never goes out without styling her hair."

"Consolation prize," I grunted. "How do we get out of here?"

Narissa ran to the corner of the room and pressed on one of the flatscreens that lined the wall. It popped away from the plaster and swung open on hinges, revealing an ominous rusted metal door.

Narissa dragged it open with both hands. The neglected hinges squealed like the jump scare in a cheap movie. The unlit stairwell beyond certainly looked like a place you'd get murdered.

"This goes to the storage on the second floor. Take the balcony all the way to the north end of the building. There are stairs that lead back to the street, and the subway entrance is right around the corner. I'll stall them as long as I can," Narissa explained.

"Perfect," I said, and ran for the stairs.

Phil tightened the straps on her backpack and followed. As she passed, Narissa grabbed her arm and held her back. "Ask for Jael. I promise she's your best bet."

I cleared my throat. It wasn't Phil who needed to be convinced.

Phil searched the woman's face. "Should I tell her you sent me?"

Narissa snorted and shoved her towards the stairs. "You don't need to namedrop me. You're Blue Fire." And then she slammed and latched the door, shutting us in the darkness.

I grabbed the railing and started up the steps, glad Phil couldn't see my expression in the shadows. Identifying herself as Blue Fire was the last thing she should be doing on the streets of Beijing. I'd find us another way out of this country, even if we had to walk to Tibet.

And if I had any say, Phil would never identify herself as Blue Fire again.

The storage room above the shop was uninhabited except for Narissa's fabric hoard. I wove around the heaps of bolts to the back entrance. After checking the peephole, I slowly lifted the deadbolt and cracked open the door.

The alley behind the building was quiet. Narissa's shop lights were still off, making the only source of light the yellowed streetlamp. I crept onto the balcony and gestured for Phil to follow. I slid along the building, careful to stay in the shadows under the awning.

A shout pierced the night. Phil choked on a gasp, slapping her hand over her mouth. I flattened myself against the building and watched. Two guards entered the far end of the alley, muttering to each other in Mandarin.

"What do we do?" Phil hissed.

"Stay quiet for starters," I reprimanded. Looking around, I spotted an abandoned brick. Moving slowly to avoid drawing attention, I shoved the brick over the edge of the balcony. It crashed onto a car below with a symphony of shattering glass.

Hopefully that wasn't Narissa's car.

The guards shouted and ran under the balcony to investigate. Taking advantage of their distraction—and the wailing car alarm—I took off at a run. "Come on!"

We raced to the north end of the building. I grasped the railing and leapt down the short metal stairs, skipping most of the steps. I didn't dare look back as we darted across the alley and around the corner, briefly exposing ourselves to the streetlights and security cameras. If we could get into the subway, we could lose them.

Phil struggled to keep up. "Don't we need a ticket?"

I shoved past a cluster of late-night commuters. "No, communism has its perks."

Phil tried to be more polite and walk around the passersby, almost losing me in the process. "But don't they scan your electronics at the gates?" she panted.

"Sure—if your devices are turned on." I led the way down the steps into the underground station, using my long legs to take two at a time. Phil clattered after me.

I shoved through the turnstile. The dead ticket scanners glared up at me wearily, their obsolete screens dark. I hurried down the long queue to the platform. The subway was closing within the hour, and the crowd on the tile was thinning. But it was still enough of a throng to get lost in.

Phil caught up to me just as the next train screeched into the station. Not trusting her to make it through the crowd, I grabbed her shoulders and pushed her onto the car ahead of me. I shoved past the other passengers and navigated to vacant seats in the far corner.

Shrugging my backpack off, I sat down. I gratefully closed my eyes and leaned my head against the window, hoping to summon a moment of silence.

Phil was oblivious to my social cues. She slid uncomfortably close to me as the train lurched away from the station. "Doesn't it trip the algorithm if you board without a device?" she hissed. She tried to lower her voice, but she only succeeded in making the pitch more irritating.

I opened my eyes for the sole purpose of rolling them dramatically. "This isn't like Boston. Fifteen million people ride the subway in Beijing every day. Even if they did try to stop you at the gate, it would be incredibly hard to determine who set off the alarm, and you could easily disappear in the crowd."

Overpopulation was the enemy of control, and Beijing's beleaguered public transportation system couldn't keep up. China didn't have the luxury of getting bogged down in paperwork and scanners like America did. That meant the subway was truly free to ride.

Of course, that grace would run out as soon as we needed to do something that involved actual money. Like buy food.

Phil accepted that explanation and scooted away, mercifully restoring some personal space. "At least we won't have any trouble getting around."

Getting around the city wasn't a problem. It was crossing the border—or worse, trying to board a plane or transit—that would take a miracle.

Phil fidgeted with her backpack straps. "Where are we going?"

I closed my eyes again and folded my arms across my chest. "Far away from here."

And that's exactly what we did. We rode the train to the end of the line, then switched to a different one and repeated the process. By the time the rails shut down, we were on the other side of the province.

We emerged into the night and walked for another half-mile. The neighborhood we found ourselves in was on the bleeding edge of modernism. The pavement was crumbling, and the storefronts were dimly lit, their cold neon signs the victims of power shortages. Up ahead, a shantytown had been razed to make room for a new trio of apartment complexes. The remains of the slum were still piled in a heap on the edge of the lot like a headstone.

Phil wisely stayed close to me as we approached the chain-link fence that blocked off the construction site. The site was not active; I could tell by the gaps in the fence and the trash blowing around the yard. Failed construction projects were a common sight in China, especially after over a hundred years of communism, and tonight that would be our salvation. An abandoned site meant no power to the security cameras.

We found a place where the fence had been cut. I held the chain link aside so Phil could slip through, then ducked in after her. I listened for signs of trouble as we hurried across the shadowy lot, but the night was quiet except for the omnipresent hum of the surrounding city.

The building was nothing more than a concrete skeleton, with no glass in the windows. A glance at the heaps of soiled blankets in the empty lobby suggested we were not the only vagrants using the shelter, but no one else was in sight. We climbed the steps to the fifth floor and claimed the first empty room. It was hardly a secure position, but at least if anyone gave us trouble, we could make a quick exit.

The room was coated in dust and littered with a few pieces of trash, but nothing obscene. I grabbed an abandoned tarp off a stack of lumber. Phil helped me shake it out and lay it in the corner, where it was sheltered from the wind.

I unclipped the wool from the backpack and handed it to her. "Get as much sleep as you can. I need you ready to run tomorrow. I'll keep watch."

She didn't argue, but her haunted eyes searched me, her pale face ghostly in the darkness. "What about you?"

I shrugged and sat down next to the doorframe. "I'm a scientist. I'm an expert at running on no sleep."

She lay down on the tarp and wrapped herself in the blanket. I stretched my long legs out, folded my arms behind my head, and propped myself on the lumpy backpack. I closed my eyes, knowing I was in no danger of falling asleep in these conditions.

Phil let me enjoy about five minutes of silence before she shattered it. "Nic?"

I didn't bother to open my eyes. "What?"

There was a pause, her breathing audible. When she spoke again, her voice was weak and labored. "I'm sorry."

I looked up and glared at the ceiling. What was I supposed to say to that? *"It's not your fault," "I forgive you," "We'll figure it out"*? None of those statements were true, and I at least had the decency not to lie to her.

I settled into the backpack. "Just get some sleep."

4: PHILADELPHIA

"Get up, we have to move!"

I started awake, although calling what I had been doing "sleeping" was perhaps being overly generous. I'd lain awake for what must have been hours, trying and failing to find the courage to talk to Nic. There was so much I wanted—needed—to say, but I knew he wasn't in the mood to hear it. So I'd put my back to him and pretended to sleep while the unspoken words cycled over and over in my head, echoing on top of one another like pressure building in a closed pot. Eventually, I'd passed out, but my emotions just turned themselves into nightmares, most of which were unembellished memories.

So when Nic shook my shoulder and yelled in my ear, I jerked into reality with a shriek and a flood of adrenaline. I nearly smacked him in the face before I realized it was him.

He saw it coming and ducked. "We need to move, now!"

"Why?" I gasped, waiting for my breathing, heart rate, vision, or literally *any* part of my body to function within normal parameters.

He yanked the blanket away from me and wadded it into a ball. "I need to get online immediately, or we're in huge trouble."

I had several follow-up questions—like how we could possibly be in any more trouble than we already were—but I knew I'd better not argue. I stumbled up and nearly fell back down again. Sleeping on concrete was making me feel like a doll whose joints had been bent out of shape by a cruel child.

Nic didn't wait for me to get it together. He slung our backpacks over his shoulder and ran for the stairs, expecting me to keep up. I tripped over debris as I crashed down the stairwell after him. When we got to the lobby, I saw movement and smelled what could have been food cooking, but Nic didn't pause to say hello. I nearly stepped on some poor old lady sleeping in a heap of plastic bags as I struggled to catch up to him.

The sky was bathed in the pale yellow of a smog-diffused sunrise. The hum of the city was louder now, like an engine without a muffler. Nic paused for only a breath to scan the yard, then darted to the hole in the fence. He slid through first, backpacks and all, and held the wire aside for me. I crawled through much less nimbly. He took off running again before I was even on my feet.

"Nic, wait!" I yelled. I willed my sluggish body to move and ran after him.

"We need to get to a shop with Wi-Fi!" he shouted back, not slowing down at all.

He whipped around the corner. I followed—and ran straight into the path of a bicycle.

The rider yelped in Mandarin and swerved. I stumbled back into the building behind me, narrowly avoiding getting my toes run over. I mumbled an apology, although I doubted the man understood me. He gave me a suspicious glare, then adjusted the sacks he had precariously balanced on his handlebars and kept moving.

Catching my breath, I looked around—and realized Nic was nowhere in sight.

Oh Jesus, help! I prayed as the panic returned like a bout of nausea. Where was he? It was early morning, but the street was already crowded. A line of several dozen commuters waiting for the bus clogged the sidewalk. Vendors congested the road with their carts, and bicyclists narrowly swerved through the mess. All around there were horns honking and signs flashing and people shouting in a language I couldn't understand—and not one of them was tall with blond hair.

"Nic!" I screeched, but it was useless. I could barely hear myself over the din.

I pressed myself against the wall as a cluster of schoolkids shoved past me. I couldn't get lost. I wouldn't last a night on my own; I didn't even have a device on me. *Where would he go? Why would he—*

The Holy Spirit breathed on me with a whisper of wisdom, causing me to stop. Nic would do exactly what he said he'd do: find a shop with public Wi-Fi. He'd look for the closest one, preferably a business where it wouldn't seem suspicious if he sat down and pulled out his laptop.

Like a café.

Thanking the Holy Spirit, I took a brave step off the curb and looked around. I couldn't read any of the signs, but it was easy to tell which stores sold food. The first two on the street were little more than kiosks with an order counter, their faded backlit menu signs nearly identical to restaurants back home. I ventured further down the road, straining to see the shops through the throng of people. *There*—I spotted a short metal fence and a cluster of rickety plastic chairs. An eatery of some kind.

I looked both ways and darted across the street. Sure enough, Nic sat at a table in an inconspicuous corner of the patio, his laptop open in front of him.

"Nic!" I shoved a vacant chair out of my way and ran to his side. I wasn't sure whether to hug him or hit him.

He barely looked up, his fingers not missing a beat as they continued to type. "Don't yell my name in public places."

"Then don't leave me behind in a public place," I snapped. The urge to hit was winning. "I almost got lost."

"*You* may have gotten lost, but I was in no danger of losing *you*." He squinted at the screen, scrolling with his finger. "You were five yards away. I was watching."

He said it like a parent supervising a toddler on the playground, and I realized that's what the whole situation must feel like to him. Except this "playground" was Beijing, and we were both wanted criminals.

"Yeah, but *I* didn't know you were watching," I argued. "I was scared."

He wasn't stirred by my emotional transparency. "You need to learn not to panic," he scolded, as if it were as simple as mastering basic multiplication. "Just slow down and think a little."

I *had* done that, not that he'd appreciate my maturity. "Well, maybe I wouldn't panic if you didn't leave me behind in Beijing!" I sighed. It was no use; he wasn't even looking at me. I pointed at the laptop. "What was so urgent, anyway?"

"Believe it or not, I have to turn in a tax form."

I didn't believe that for a second. "I thought you hated paperwork."

He hit enter. "My point exactly."

None of this made any sense. Since when were taxes urgent? What government form could possibly be so important that he'd risk going online? Surely our files were marked by now.

"Never mind," I said aloud, in case he was thinking about being forthcoming with more information. "If you're going to make a mark online, I might as well buy some food."

"Excellent idea." He pulled his phone out of his pocket and tossed it at me. "Go to the shop next door. Get some packaged food, fruit—anything that will travel well."

"Sure." I slung my little black backpack over my shoulder—just in case—and unzipped the bag Narissa had given us. I spied an empty shopping sack made of silk remnants and a metal canteen and grabbed both.

"Don't turn the phone on until you're ready to pay," Nic continued his safety lecture, "and then come straight back here." His eyes left his screen for a minute. "I promise I'm watching."

I didn't grace that with a response. I turned and navigated around the metal fence to the shop next door. It was a little corner store, its front display crammed to the overflowing with ramen. I stepped through the open door and blinked. The place was surreally bright, washed out by the white walls and the blinding lights from the row of refrigerator cases. I wandered up the aisles, scanning the colorful packages decorated with cute cartoons. I couldn't read any Mandarin, but thankfully most of the labels had pictures—some were even written in English. I filled my bag with a variety of ready-to-eat food and hoped Nic wouldn't criticize my shopping skills.

I reached the back of the store and saw the drink station. There was a soda fountain and a futuristic smoothie maker—and a carafe of fresh coffee. I grinned, twisted the cap off my canteen, and filled it to the brim.

The clerk, a gentle-looking old man, put his tablet down when I approached. I offered him a smile and unloaded my purchases on the counter. I hoped he wouldn't think me rude for not talking.

I put my canteen on the counter. He nodded at it. "Coffee?" he asked.

"Yes, please," I said, taking advantage of the moment to speak in English.

He winked and hit a key on his terminal. The payment kiosk on the edge of the counter flickered to life, a total displayed on the screen.

I powered on Nic's phone. The payment app—the universal way to legally transfer money in the United—was right on the home page. I held my phone over the kiosk and hesitated. As soon as I made this purchase, Asia, if she was watching Nic's file, would know exactly where we were. But we needed food, so there was no way around it.

I tapped the phone to the kiosk and braced myself, subconsciously expecting it to cough up an error. It didn't. The screen turned green, and a happy smiling face appeared, praising me for my responsible citizenship.

The clerk started to hand my purchases back to me—then stopped. He squinted at his terminal. "Is not your phone."

I couldn't tell whether he meant it as a question or a statement, but I didn't know how to answer him. How did he know it wasn't my phone? Did it pull up Nic's ID on his screen? Some stores in America could see your ID after you paid. If that was the case, there was no way I'd pass for mustached Dr. Nic Von Nieuwenhuyse, so I decided to opt for a half-truth.

"No, it's my… dad's," I managed, and grimaced. I held the phone below the counter and powered it off.

The clerk squinted at me, then relented. He shoved the rest of my packages across the counter towards me. I shoveled them into my bag, thanked him, and ran out the door, almost forgetting my canteen.

Nic was still typing aggressively on his laptop. "Yay, you survived," he deadpanned.

I ignored the shot. "Are you ready to go?" I asked, standing uncomfortably close to his chair. Maybe if I hovered in his bubble, he'd catch my sense of urgency.

He elbowed me away. "Almost. I forgot how many forms were involved in this. It's been a long time since I married someone."

I dropped the canteen. It hit the brick with a loud *thunk* and rolled under the table. "You got *married?*"

"Sorry, poor choice of words." He kicked the canteen back towards me. "I meant I *officiated* a wedding."

That was no less shocking. Nic was the least romantic person in the galaxy, and when would he have had time to officiate a wedding? Who in the world that we knew was getting married right now? "Who—"

I didn't get to finish the question. Just then, the clerk from the corner store approached us—followed by several younger, bigger, meaner-looking men.

The clerk gave me a reproachful frown, like I'd stolen a candy bar. "This is your dad?" He nodded at Nic.

Nic slammed the laptop shut and glared at me. "What did you tell him?"

Now did not seem like the time to explain. I grabbed the canteen off the ground and backed away. "Sorry, sirs, we were just going."

Nic took the cue and started to stand up. One of the younger men clamped a hand on his shoulder and pushed him back down.

The clerk folded his arms and barked something in Mandarin. I was more than a little surprised when Nic spat back in the same language.

"What did he say?" I asked.

Nic rolled his eyes, as if this was a perfectly normal exchange to have with strangers. "They're performing a citizen's arrest on me."

5: NIC

Phil tried and failed to land a reaction to that.

"And what did you say?" she finally managed.

"Over my dead body."

I swung my long legs and knocked the clerk flat on his back. His old bones cracked on the brick, drawing gasps from the passersby, but there was no time to waste on sympathy. The young grunts he had with him tried to hold me down, but I whipped my holstered gun from underneath my jacket.

The weapon wasn't on, but the boys wisely didn't take the time to find out. They scattered, cursing. I returned the sentiment as I stood up and kicked my chair at them. At least that would give them something to trip over.

Phil, to her credit, turned and ran without being told. I grabbed my laptop and backpack and caught up to her in three strides.

We darted across the street. The noise of the crowd changed pitch as bystanders registered what was happening. A path cleared in front of us thanks to my brandished gun, but there were shouts and screams in our direction. I saw the flash of a cellphone camera and knew we had to get out of sight before the entire internet knew we were here.

"Should we take the subway?" Phil yelled.

"No, it's rush hour—we'll get stuck in the line. This way!" I concealed my gun and pointed towards the next row of shops. We jumped up on the sidewalk, narrowly missing a bus as it screeched to a stop. I shoved my way through the line of commuters, eliciting complaints. Phil stumbled along in my wake.

I darted through the nearest gap in the buildings to the alleyway behind. It was almost as busy as the street itself, with neighbors gossiping in back doorways and several rear-facing shop entrances. I kept one eye on the uneven road as I led us around tent signs and abandoned mopeds. Phil clutched her shopping bag to her chest and managed to keep up.

We ran to the end of the row, then slipped between the buildings to the next street over. We repeated this process, zigzagging between blocks, until we were at least a mile from our original location.

I halted when I reached the end of the street. Phil rear-ended me. "What are you doing?" she hissed.

"Acting natural," I returned. I smoothed my hair and strolled onto the main road like I had nowhere to be. Phil imitated me, albeit poorly. I paused at the first shop and pretended to browse the wares, even as my eyes scanned the street. The crowd flowed around us calmly. There were no stares or cameras being aimed in our direction, and I couldn't hear any commotion over the normal din of traffic. So far, this side of town was none the wiser to our disturbance.

We'd gotten lucky. But luck had a nasty habit of refusing to repeat itself.

I shouldered my backpack and continued walking. "Keep up."

She scampered to obey. "Why did they try to arrest you?"

"Besides my criminal good looks? That's an excellent question. What in the world happened in there?" I glared down at her. She had barely been out of my sight for five minutes, and she'd managed to blow our cover while buying potato chips. I knew Phil wasn't very street-smart, but that level of incompetence was stupendous even for her.

"I don't know!" She almost dropped the canteen as she struggled to hold on to her purchases. "Everything went fine. I paid without issue, and he seemed nice. He even spoke English."

"So what, you struck up a conversation about how I'm an amazing parent?" The very word left a bad taste in my mouth. "Did you really tell the guy I was your father?"

She stopped in the middle of the sidewalk. "*That's* what you're worried about?"

I turned to face her. "Obviously, or I wouldn't be asking."

She must be getting hungry, because her tolerance for sarcasm was even lower than usual. "You're the one who called me your 'daughter' in front of Jayde," she snapped.

I didn't need to be reminded. "I was going for dramatic." I'd been trying to strike the fear of God into my enemies—and I'd succeeded quite well, judging by the fact that Jayde had immediately lost control of the situation.

"Well, I was going for believable." She crossed her arms and pouted. "He asked me if the phone was mine, and I figured it must have pulled up your ID or something. So I lied. And legally, that wasn't a lie."

It wasn't, but I didn't need to be reminded of that either. "The technical term is 'legal guardian,' but..." I sighed. In her defense, she'd handled the situation as well as could be expected, but this little revelation confirmed the worst. "Well, at least that explains one thing."

"What?" she asked.

After glancing around to make sure no passersby had suddenly become interested in our conversation, I confessed: "Asia must have flagged my file as a national security risk."

She gaped at me with that stupid bug-eyed expression I hated so much. "Meaning?"

"Meaning that if I check in anywhere, not only will it alert the government, but it will also alert nearby citizens and authorize them to detain me. It's a security code normally used for terrorists and escaped convicts—or people you really want to catch."

To be fair, according to Asia, I fit all three of those categories.

Phil bit her lip so hard it flushed white. "So no more buying food."

"So no more buying food." Or making phone calls. Or crossing any checkpoint that required a thumb scan. I knew we'd have to be sparing with our online activity; Asia was undoubtedly watching our files like a hawk, waiting for us to give her a pinpoint so she could pounce. Now, she wouldn't even have to hurry. If we checked in anywhere, the patriotic citizens of Beijing would detain us until she got there.

And as much as I believed in the power of a good gun, even I knew that "eat, shoot and leave" wasn't a long-term solution.

"I'm sorry," Phil mumbled.

I rubbed my neglected mustache. There were plenty of things about our situation that I could blame Phil for, but this wasn't one of them. I should have checked my file before logging in at a crowded place.

My thought trailed off when I realized the math of the situation wasn't adding up. Why had it taken the crowd so long to notice us? No one had been suspicious until Phil paid using my phone. I'd been online with the laptop for a good ten, maybe fifteen minutes, and no one had said anything. If Andromeda's file was flagged as mine was, then the owner of the shop whose Wi-Fi I borrowed—as well as all the patrons at nearby tables— should have gotten an alert.

Unless...

I ducked into the shadows of the nearest alley, sat down on a back step, and pulled out my laptop.

"What are you doing?" Phil screeched at a delightful pitch. She darted to my side and hovered in my bubble like she always did when she was nervous. "You just said we couldn't go online."

"*I* can't. But you..." The shop's Wi-Fi was just strong enough for me to connect from the alley. I pulled up Andromeda's file and proved myself right: She hadn't been flagged, at least not with any public alerts. Asia was no doubt tracking her, but as far as the rest of the world was concerned, Andromeda was still a citizen in good standing.

I angled the screen so Phil could see. Her jaw went slack like she'd been stabbed with a needle. "That doesn't make any sense."

I agreed, it didn't—and I hated when things didn't make sense. Most of my enemies could be decoded, their behavior reduced to an algorithm dependent on what they had to win or lose. But there was nothing more dangerous than a villain with hidden motivations. People like that could not be controlled, and when I couldn't control the game, I almost always lost.

I'd never been able to control Asia. And to think a younger, more idealistic version of myself had found that attractive.

"Maybe she's hoping I'll keep checking in online so she can use me to find you," Phil suggested.

"You're not that stupid," I countered, and hoped she wouldn't prove me wrong. "It would be much faster to flag your file and let the authorities find you. Then she could just torture you until I got bored of listening to you scream and turned myself in."

"Classy," Phil grunted, and she wasn't wrong. Asia truly had created the perfect trap. Even if I wanted to send Phil home and flee on my own—something I would do in a heartbeat—I couldn't. Asia would find Phil and use her as bait to lure me in.

But if Phil was supposed to be the lump of peanut butter in the mousetrap, why not flag her file? It would be so much more efficient to let Beijing's surveillance state do the heavy lifting. Asia didn't like getting dirt under her fingernails; all this manual labor was not her style.

No, if Asia was going to the trouble of keeping Phil's file clean, that meant she had a very specific reason for doing so. She needed Phil for something.

I froze when I realized my fatal error. Phil wasn't the bait in the mousetrap.

I was.

6: PHILADELPHIA

Nic glared at the screen in silence, long enough that I began to worry. Admittedly, with how frayed my nerves were, it was a short trip.

"Is something wrong?" I prodded.

He slammed the laptop shut and stood up. "Give me the phone," he demanded, ignoring the question.

I fished it out of my pocket. He took it and typed with both thumbs. "I'm registering this phone to you, so we can at least buy food without getting arrested. But Asia is watching your file, so we can only check in if absolutely necessary."

"What if Asia updates my security code?"

"She won't," he declared unequivocally.

He was probably right, but that still raised several insidious questions. Nic might disagree, but I knew Asia was keeping my file clean to try to bribe me into coming home. That had been her M.O. since we'd met. She would ignore any sin and bend any law as long as I agreed to be Andromeda Nolan.

Had she really done all that just to trap Nic? I wasn't sure I believed that. She'd gone to an awful lot of trouble to induct me into high society, even going so far as to decorate my bedroom at the Nolans' Beijing estate. Hiring an interior designer seemed like an excess if all she wanted was her ex-boyfriend back.

But then again, I had no idea what her history was with Nic. Surely, she wanted a lot more than romance from him, but now was definitely not the time to ask Nic about his love life.

The device screeched at him. "I'm taking this offline so we can turn it on without triggering an alert. I want you to keep it on you in case we get separated, but do *not* bring it online unless I give you express permission."

I nodded. "Right."

He held the phone out. I went to take it, but he refused to let go, forcing me to look up at him.

He stared at me for a beat before speaking. "I'm trusting you."

"I know." I met his gaze.

His gray eyes darkened like an impending storm. "Really? Because the last time we had a bonding moment like this, you immediately turned around and ignored all my advice."

I looked at my muddy boots as his words dragged my spirits down like a rock under water. "Nic..." I started, but there was nothing to say. He'd made himself clear. He said he trusted me—but he didn't.

He let go of the phone. I stared at my reflection on the dark screen as the weight settled in my hands like a live bomb.

"We need to keep moving—they'll know we checked in here." He turned and led the way down the alley.

I pocketed the phone and followed him. I waited until we'd reached the end of the block before attempting conversation. "Where are we going?"

"Out of the city. We need to get somewhere rural where there isn't as much surveillance."

I quickened my pace to match his long strides. "But what about Jael?"

He gave that tired groan that made me regret I'd said anything. "I'm sure she's a charming individual, but I am not in the mood for a ghost hunt."

"But Narissa said—"

"Narissa hasn't even met her." Nic looked down at me, but the condescending expression on his face made me wish he wouldn't. "Andi, we are not risking our lives for a phantom. We know nothing about this woman, if she even exists. And you of all people know what happens when you trust someone you don't know."

I turned my attention to the cluttered street ahead of us so he couldn't see the tears that abruptly stung my eyes. Maybe it was because I was hungry, and everything still hurt, and I had a headache, and I probably should have stopped to drink water seventeen blocks ago—but suddenly, I just wanted this conversation to be over. I didn't want to be reminded that we were in this mess because I trusted someone I shouldn't have.

And yet, even as I tried to wade through the guilt, I knew I wouldn't be alive right now if I hadn't trusted certain people along the way: Cea, Stanyard, John and Dowe, even Nic. *Especially* Nic. A few months ago, I'd had every reason not to trust Nic. But I'd given him a chance, and he'd never made me regret that choice. Even now, when he was being tactless and cold, I still didn't regret letting him into my life.

What was the difference? What separated Nic from someone like Jayde? Neither of them knew Jesus, at least not in any appreciable way. Nic had walked away from his parents' faith years ago and never looked back. He'd also kidnapped my brother, threatened my father, tried to invent a superweapon, and various other sundry crimes. So why could I trust him and not Jayde? How was I supposed to know who to trust in the future? What was I supposed to be looking for?

Unfortunately, Nic didn't seem interested in educating me on the nuances. He strode into the intersection, barely pausing to look for oncoming traffic. "If we can get somewhere rural," he continued seamlessly, "I should be able to make a call without giving Asia a direct pinpoint—or I might be able to find someone who's willing to help us launder money so I can buy fake prints. If I can just get online without tipping Asia off, I can call your brother or that boyfriend of yours and—"

"Stanyard!" I gasped, causing Nic to jump. I hadn't meant to shout, but I'd just remembered that I'd texted Stanyard the night before. Surely, he'd replied by now.

I stepped up on the sidewalk and pulled the phone out. "What are you doing?" Nic demanded, reaching for me.

I jerked back. "I'm just seeing if he replied. If there are any new messages, they would have downloaded while you were online. I'm not going to text him back—Nic, do you really think I'm that stupid?"

He folded his arms. "You're a teenage girl in love. Yes, I think you're that stupid."

I growled and turned away from him. My relationship with Stanyard was one of the few good things that had happened since I'd come back to Earth. Why did Nic have to be so mean about it?

Why did he have to be so mean about everything?

I opened the messaging app and was rewarded with a dozen messages from Stanyard. The first few were the usual somersault of *you're okay I was so worried I miss you I'm so sorry this happened I love you.* I couldn't help but smile even as my heart ached; Stanyard always rambled when he panicked.

When he realized I wasn't online and responding, he'd slowed down and started using fewer words. He confirmed he was safe and told me to take care of myself and not worry about him. Then he sent the message I really needed to hear:

I KNOW WHY YOU WENT. I WANT YOU TO KNOW I FORGIVE YOU.

The screen blurred as my eyes swam with tears, welcome ones this time. I'd known, factually, that he would forgive me. We'd been through too much over the past two months, had too many fallouts and apologies, for this to be the last straw. He'd forgiven me even when I couldn't forgive myself.

I could only hope he still loved me even though I absolutely didn't love myself.

I scrolled to the last message.

I SAW THE LIVESTREAM. I'M PROUD OF YOU.

I closed my eyes and took a deep breath, letting his words put a period on my anxiety. At least *someone* thought I did the right thing.

I looked up to find Nic still staring at me. "What? Do you want to read the messages?" I shook the device at him.

He put his hands up. "No thank you. I've got enough on my plate dealing with Asia's unrequited love—I don't need to add your teenage hormones to the list."

"Good, I didn't want your opinion anyway," I returned, then regretted it. It was a rude thing to say—and it wasn't even true. I *did* want Nic's opinion. I just didn't want the biting sarcasm and cruel disinterest that usually came with it.

Nic gracelessly changed the subject. "What's for breakfast?"

More like brunch at this point. I shoved the shopping bag at him.

He took it and riffled through the contents. "Let's find a place to sit—I need to plan our route."

We turned the corner and found ourselves in an arts district. Bronze statues cluttered the sidewalk, and carefully curated graffiti coated every available wall. Across the square, a series of historic brick buildings had been converted into a gallery. The roofs were a strange scallop design paneled with glass, and the remains of a smokestack stuck into the sky—a decommissioned factory of sorts. I could tell at a glance that much of the art was brazenly political, praising the United and its communist predecessors, but at least the place was a tourist trap. It was decently busy, with plenty of Americans milling around, so we wouldn't stand out.

We found a secluded park bench and sat with our backs to a brick wall. Nic unwrapped a protein bar and started gnawing on it, propping both elbows on his knees and staring into space like he always did when he was processing.

I fished out the canteen. The metal was still slightly warm to the touch, making me hope the contents were still hot. I unscrewed the lid and took a slow sip. It tasted different from the coffee Mrs. Von, Nic's mom, made, but it was still coffee. It was familiar, normal—and normalcy was something I desperately needed right now.

I inhaled the earthy steam and tried to imagine myself back in Boston. Normally at this time, I'd be sitting at the Vons' kitchen island, listening to Mr. Von's good-natured chatter while a mundane sitcom droned on the TV in the background. Mrs. Von would be bustling about the kitchen, opening every cabinet in the room until she found the plates that had been on the same shelf for the last twenty years.

Thanks to a botched neurosurgery—another cruel government attempt to crush the unassimilated—the Vons had the object permanence of a six-month-old. They forgot everything as soon as it was out of sight. No doubt they'd forgotten about me by now, moved on and created a new daily routine as if I'd never existed.

I'd give anything for the pleasure of reintroducing myself.

Would I ever see them again? Going back to Boston seemed impossible. The government was just as controlling there as it was here, and I couldn't trust the underground, not after what happened with Jayde. The assassination had been a blackout mission; only a handful of people even knew I was in Beijing. But I had no way of knowing who was on Jayde's side and who was on mine. And if Jayde managed to get out of Beijing alive, he may very well poison the rest of them against me.

I reached up and instinctively rubbed my right shoulder, where my thunderbird tattoo was hidden under my sleeve. What did the internet think of me now? A week ago, I'd been a trending celebrity, the figurehead of a revolution. My videos raked in millions of views as Jayde used my image—the thunderbird—to coordinate Operation Blue Fire.

We'd been months away from staging a global demonstration designed to wake the public from their stupor, but now what? In my last video, I'd told my followers I was going offline while some stuff blew over. I'd intended to reveal myself to the world when I killed the General. What would people say if I didn't come online for weeks? Would Operation Blue Fire still happen without me?

The unassimilated—social noncompliants who refused to deny their religious and national identities and sign the file—were still in danger. The leadership in Beijing was planning to deport all the unassimilated to work camps in China, a certain one-way trip. If Operation Blue Fire didn't succeed, what would happen to my people—the Christians, the Jews, the rejects? If we lost the momentum of the revolution, there would be no getting it back. And if my feud with Jayde divided us from the inside, we'd be worse off than when we started.

And it would, as always, be my fault.

7: NIC

I'd get so much more done if I didn't spend half my waking hours saving Phil from her own thoughts.

She'd gone silent—the kind of silence where she forgets to breathe—disrupting the atmospheric pressure and jerking me out of my mind palace. I looked up and saw that she was two beats away from a meltdown. Her shoulders were hunched and her face was pinched like she was caving in on herself. I could tell by the look in her eyes that she was trapped in a cycle of guilt and unanswered questions. I knew what would happen if she crashed at the bottom, and I was not about to spend the rest of my day putting her back together.

"What's in the canteen?" I interrupted.

She abruptly relaxed her grip, almost dropping it. She held it out to me.

I got a whiff of the contents, and suddenly, life became significantly less horrible.

I snatched the canteen and gulped the coffee like it was oxygen itself. The rich, still-warm liquid hit my throat, putting my soul back in my body. I felt my humanity returning; maybe I could actually get through today without murdering something.

I came up for air with a satisfied sigh. "You're hired."

She regarded me with amusement. "For what?"

"My assistant."

She paused and gave my offhand comment way too much thought. "That's actually a job I could probably handle."

"Well, we've already established you can fetch coffee." That was half the job description. "Can you reply to emails and manage a calendar?"

She shrugged. "I mean, sure."

"And can you keep secrets from the government?"

"With pleasure."

I gave her a sideways glance. "Except for that one time you turned my entire base over to Ambrose."

It took her so long to get the joke that I almost regretted making it.

"Wow," she finally managed after she'd gaped at me for a solid minute.

"What? Too soon?"

"No, I... I'm just surprised you know how to tease." She leaned away, as if she were afraid I was going to take it back.

I shrugged and took another drink of coffee. "It's just sarcasm but nicer."

She grinned and held out her hand for the canteen.

I passed it to her in surprise. "You like black coffee?"

She tipped the canteen back and chugged like a drunk pirate. "Is there another way to take it?"

There wasn't—and there was only one person who could have taught her that.

Her dad didn't drink the stuff. Her brother used enough cream that he may as well start with a gallon of milk and add a splash of coffee to it. Even my dad took some sugar with his.

No, she definitely learned this important life skill from me. And, if she was picking up on my sense of humor and coffee drinking habits, logical deduction assumed that she was also learning other things from me.

It took me a full five minutes to reboot my universe around that unfortunate fact.

We ate in silence for a while. Phil nibbled on a bag of trail mix, eating one piece at a time like she had to make it last. I chewed on another protein bar, struggling to keep my thoughts on our present predicament.

Normally, I possessed an inhuman ability to hyperfocus on a problem until I found a solution. But no matter how many times I started over at the beginning and tried to trace our next steps, my mind kept wandering off like an untrained dog. Asia, my parents, the base on Mars, the fragile teenage girl sitting next to me—my thoughts insisted on focusing on anything *but* the most immediate problem.

Perhaps it was because I subconsciously knew there was no solution. At least no solution that I liked.

After about ten minutes, I could tell Phil wanted to break the silence, so I let her. "What's wrong?" I said by way of invitation.

She drummed her fingers on the bench. "Can I tell you something?"

Always would have been the correct answer, but I opted to be a little less sappy. "That's certainly preferable to keeping it stuffed up inside."

She snorted, then paused to parse her words. "Sometimes... sometimes I wish I hadn't blown up that lab in Wing 74."

I blinked. When I didn't respond for a long moment, she arched an eyebrow. "Sorry," I coughed, "that was just a deeper personal revelation than I was prepared for. Run that by me again?"

"I mean... I know it was the right thing to do. I don't *regret* it. But like... sometimes I think about how living in Wing 74 would have been so much easier than dealing with all this. Putting up with you would have been... easy."

"Solid burn. Thank you for confirming that I utterly failed as an evil overlord."

She giggled, and the sound was less annoying than I would have expected. "I guess... I just finally understand how Ephesus could do it. How he could put up with that for two years, you know?"

I did know, partially because I'd designed it that way. But I also knew that compromise like that led down a very dangerous path. Compromise had made her brother a coward. It had killed her father. And it had turned me into the kind of man who would kidnap, murder, and set the world on fire.

I tapped my foot and ordered my words carefully. "You want to hear something equally personal and awkward?"

She looked up at me and waited.

I met her gaze. "I'm glad you blew up that lab."

Her whole face lit up—probably, I noted in retrospect, because she had been waiting to hear those words for a very long time. "Really?"

I nodded. "If you hadn't, your father would have created Red Rain, and I would have given it to Carnegie, who would have given it to Thames, and Asia would have gotten what she wanted all along."

It was the truth. But as I stared at Philadelphia, with her big, watery doe-eyes that I used to hate so much, I realized that might not be the only reason.

She smiled, but the warm fuzzy feelings were short-lived. "So, you and Asia..."

"Oh, here we go," I groaned. I rubbed my temples and tried to psych myself up for the conversation I'd been avoiding for nearly a decade. "Let's just get this all out of the way. Yes, we dated once. No, we were never married. Yes, she was just as terrible a person then as she is now. And no, I'm not still in love with her. End of story."

"Okay, but you did love her once," Phil clarified.

"I should have known that's the part of the story you'd get hung up on."

"I just don't understand... *how*. Why?"

"Why? Besides the fact that she was an attractive woman?"

Still is, unfortunately.

"Nic," Phil scolded.

"What? I was a young man once, believe it or not."

She folded her arms and glared at me. I knew she wouldn't leave me alone until I gave her the full story, so I relented and leaned back against the wall. "She was powerful... and rich. She could bend laws, forge files, and get any paperwork approved."

"And?" Phil prodded.

"And what?" I sighed. This story was going to go on forever if she kept questioning my answers.

"And there has to be something more. You're not that shallow."

It was almost a compliment if I thought about it hard enough. "I was then."

I begrudgingly dredged up the memories and tried to resurrect the boy I'd been when I'd met Asia nearly fifteen years ago. It wasn't as difficult as I would have liked. He was still there, lurking in the back of my mind like a deadbeat in his parents' basement. I'd suffocated him over the years with sarcasm and plans of world domination, but he was still very much alive.

"I was trying to create Red Rain and needed someone to cut the red tape. Asia gave me everything I wanted: unlimited funding and complete freedom from government scrutiny. All in exchange for the low, low price of love and companionship."

Phil twitched her nose like a rabbit as she chewed on that information. "Why? Did she really like you that much?"

So much for giving me compliments. "I think she wanted to watch the world burn as much as I did." Asia had made it very clear that she wanted to break the system. My mistake was believing that she wanted to do it for the same reasons.

"And you?"

I stared up at the sky as that foolish little boy reared his head out of the basement. "I believed it could be done."

I'd truly believed that Red Rain could change the system—and that Asia was the one to do it with me. We'd been unstoppable in our heyday. With her connections and influence, and my charisma and science, there was no sponsor we could not win, no official we could not manipulate. We could have done it. We could have saved the world.

Of course, back then there was still something—someone—in the world worth saving.

There was a pause, and then Phil asked the question I'd been dreading most of all. "What happened?"

I took a deep breath, knowing full well this revelation would fundamentally alter her opinion of me in a way I wasn't sure I was ready for. "I refused to give her Red Rain."

Phil jerked upright and nearly fell off the bench. "You—what?"

"Surprise," I droned. "I wanted to abandon the project, but she wouldn't have it."

Phil tried and failed to adjust to this new reality. "But how... why... You literally faked people's deaths to keep this project a secret. That makes no sense for you."

"It didn't then, either."

"But... what changed your mind?"

"My dad."

The same person who had always possessed the power to change my mind—the one catalyst who had repeatedly disrupted the chemical equation of my life.

Her expression brightened at the mention of him, then immediately fell again. "He knew?"

"Dads know everything," I muttered, a fact she hadn't quite figured out yet. "He tried to convince me to stop—told me there was a better way."

"There is a better way," Phil echoed.

I turned away and stared at one of the uninspired statues across the plaza. There were many reasons why I'd never wanted to have this conversation with Phil, but that was at the top of the list. I knew she'd say the same things my dad used to, partly because they were practically the same person.

After all, Phil was the only other person who had ever convinced me to change my mind about Red Rain.

With an uncharacteristic amount of discretion, Phil decided not to push it. She stared at her lap, tracing the scratches in the metal canteen with her chipped fingernail. I knew she was running the numbers and searching for the missing piece in my tragic life story.

I waited. She'd get there in a second.

"Asia was the one who did it," she declared after a moment. She looked up at me for confirmation. "Asia put your parents under."

"Bingo. She thought it would convince me why we needed Red Rain. I think she was hoping it would be my villain origin story."

I winced. Even I could tell that there was too much pain in my voice for the sarcasm to be effective, so I gave up. "Unfortunately for her, I hacked into the medical records and found out who authorized the procedure."

I remembered the blinding rage, the nauseous grief, the shattering of ceramic as I'd hurled my coffee mug into the wall. And through it all, a seeping tidal wave of guilt as I realized I was a complete and utter failure.

Phil hesitated. She regarded me nervously, her jaw set on edge like she always did when she was afraid to tell me something. "What?" I said, even though I was quite sure I didn't want to know.

"She succeeded," she whispered.

"Who did?"

"Asia. She won." Phil swallowed and pushed the rest of the words out. "Putting your parents through surgery *did* inspire you to finish Red Rain. She got what she wanted."

My vision flashed black and blue as I realized she was right. It may not have gone the way she'd hoped, but Asia had still won in the end. She'd faded into the shadows and waited patiently for eight years while I created Red Rain for her.

It was my fault for not realizing she was still watching. In truth, she'd never left. She'd given me some space, letting my former assistant Carnegie and her cohort Thames run the show so I wouldn't think it was her. But she'd always been there, waiting, playing the long game, keeping the government off my scent so I could give her the keys to the apocalypse.

I'd always known I was a fool for getting involved with Asia. But it wasn't until now that I realized what an idiot I truly was.

Phil interrupted my self-flagellation. "Do you think she still wants Red Rain?"

I shook my head. "If she did, she'd have it already. She's known about 'Andromeda' this whole time. If she wanted to use you as blackmail to bribe your father, she would have done that two months ago. Even now, if she really wants the formula, she can just run a brain scan on him."

"But…" Phil started, not as an argument, but as a plea for reassurance that her father was safe.

I wasn't about to lie to her. "We've been over this. If any of your father's memories are intact, that includes Red Rain. All she has to do is hook him up to a synaptic device, and she can download everything she wants to know."

That had probably been Asia's plan all along. Dr. Smyrna was Phil's biological father and the real scientist responsible for making Red Rain a reality. My former assistant Carnegie had kidnapped him and had him cryogenically frozen—one of the many preventable tragedies that had happened because Phil ignored my advice. Carnegie had been planning to sell the body— and the formula for Red Rain—to Asia.

And then, inexplicably, Asia's plans had changed. Phil had interrupted the deal and made a mess of things, as she often did, but it was nothing Asia couldn't have fixed. If Asia wanted Dr. Smyrna's body, she could have procured it by now. She'd been watching Phil and knew she'd been staying with my parents; all Asia would have had to do was send a car to follow Phil, and she could have snatched the old man like taking an egg out of a nest.

No, I believed Asia when she said she didn't need Red Rain anymore, and that was the most insidious revelation about this whole ordeal. Red Rain had outlived its usefulness. Asia had a new plan, and all I knew was that her plan involved Philadelphia.

Unfortunately for her, Philadelphia was the one thing I wouldn't let her have.

8: PHILADELPHIA

Nic fell silent. Without even finishing his last thought, he propped his elbows on his knees and returned to the depths of his mind.

I let him go. I turned my focus back to my forgotten lunch and tried to find the center of my own thoughts in the bottom of the trail mix bag.

Like a finished jigsaw puzzle, Nic's story explained everything. All the events and characters that had intersected our lives over the last nine months lined up like pieces on a chess board. Clearly, Asia had been controlling this game of chess for a very long time, and my family and I were just the latest pawns in her army.

And yet, the truth of Nic's past was completely dissonant from the caricature I'd built in my mind. Perhaps without realizing it, I'd written my own explanation to Nic's behavior, a twisted backstory that helped me justify the mad scientist who had become my ally.

I'd assumed until today that Nic had always been amoral, a man without a compass or regard for human life. That's how

Ephesus had described him, although my brother had definitely seen Nic at his worst. But even Cea had made it sound like her brother had always been this way—aloof, coldhearted, and willing to sacrifice those he loved.

But maybe neither of them had ever met the real Nic. The Nic who listened to his father's advice. The Nic who wasn't afraid to stand up to Asia. The Nic who abandoned Red Rain because he believed there was a better way.

That was the Nic I knew.

It made me wonder if Nic knew more about God than he cared to admit. After all, Nic's parents were diehard Christians; the apple can only fall so far from the tree, even if that apple is actively trying to roll away down the hill. I also knew Nic had a soft side, however much he hated it. For someone who had been bent on starting WWIV less than a year ago, he hadn't been very hard to convert.

If I of all people could convince Nic to change his mind, then it must have been a short trip.

There was so much I wanted to ask him, but I figured I had exhausted his emotional transparency for one day, so I held my tongue. Instead, I closed my eyes and did something I probably should have been doing all along: I prayed for him.

Nic crumpled his wrapper and stood up. "We should keep moving."

I groaned. I was already starting to hate that phrase, and it wasn't even noon.

We deposited our trash and left the arts district. Nic offered to carry the shopping bag, so I let him. The sun was now high overhead, blanketing the city in a layer of mugginess that was almost as thick as the smog itself. I stripped my leather jacket and tied it around my waist. I felt sorry for Nic; he rolled up the sleeves of his windbreaker, but he couldn't take it off unless he wanted to cause a scene with his holstered gun. I could tell he was uncomfortable, with a line of sweat dampening the edge of his greasy blond hair.

Descending into the subway tunnel brought us some relief. Rush hour had dwindled, so while there was still a sizable queue clogging the platform, the line at least appeared to be moving. We waited until three trains had come and gone before we finally found room on a car.

I grabbed the hem of Nic's jacket as the crowd squeezed us onto the train. It felt like we were being carried along, like a branch dragged with the current. People bustled against me on all sides, rubbing against my arm and digging my backpack into my shoulder blades. It was hot and noisy, and all I could see was a blur of foreign faces. I held my breath, afraid that if I let it out, there wouldn't be enough air for me to get another.

Suddenly, we broke through a gap to the interior of the car. I stumbled into Nic as the train lurched into motion. Thankfully, he was tall enough to grab the top bar, so I held onto him as he stood steady. I refused to let go as he weaseled our way further into the car; every time someone would move, he'd slide in to take their place.

After about fifteen minutes, we managed to snatch a seat in the corner. There was only one, and Nic all but shoved me into it when the occupier got up to make their stop.

"Thanks," I said, reaching to take the shopping bag from him.

He just nodded as he stationed himself in front of me, grabbing the bar above my head.

I watched out the window as the train sped up. The lights of the tunnel blurred into a streak, then abruptly came back into focus again as the train slowed at the next platform. I waited until we'd passed three more stops before speaking again.

"End of the line?" I ventured.

He grunted. "This line goes all the way to the west side of the province. We'll get off there, see about catching a bus out of the district."

I traced the embroidery on the silk bag and didn't respond. I didn't want to question him, but I wasn't sure getting out of the city would do us any good. Nic couldn't log in anywhere, and if I went online, it would give Asia a beacon to find us both. Even if the location wasn't precise, it would still tell her what village we were in, and it might be more difficult for us to hide in the country than it was in the city. The further we got into the rural areas, the fewer Americans there would be, and the more we'd stand out. Especially Nic—even in the subway car, he was at least a head above most of the other riders.

But even if we could get online, what then? Thanks to the inheritance Thames Nolan had left to me, I was rich, but I couldn't spend a penny without leaving a digital trail. We needed to launder money, but I doubted some poor rice farmer in the middle of the mountains could—or would—help us with that. Nic said he was going to call Ephesus, but what could my brother do? He was a hundred million miles away on Mars.

I winced. What must my brother think? I hadn't involved him in any of this. He'd been offline on a transit to Mars during this whole ordeal. He'd been supportive of my role as Blue Fire, just like he had supported me my entire life, but I could tell he didn't like the idea of me leading a revolution any more than Nic did. I'm sure he was horrified when he found out I'd gone to China with the intent of murdering a man. And now I'd dropped off the grid completely; I hadn't even sent him a text when I was last online.

I looked up at Nic. "Have you talked to Ephesus?"

The glazed look in his eyes shattered. "Oh—" He started to swear, then caught himself just in time.

I stiffened, instantly resuming panic mode. "What?"

He aggressively rubbed his face with his hand. "There's something you should know."

I tried to swallow, but it caught in my throat. "I hate it when you say that."

"You and me both."

I braced my feet on the floor as the subway screeched to a stop at the next platform. "Is Ephesus okay?"

"Oh, he's doing *fantastic.*" The bitterness in Nic's voice was so palpable that you could have snapped a piece off like peanut brittle.

I took a deep breath and tried to remind my heart that things really couldn't get any worse at this point. "Well, just as long as no one's dead, getting adopted, or changing their name."

Nic grimaced. "We're good on the first two. But there might be a name change involved."

"What?" Abruptly, the events of this morning snapped into focus. "Wait, does this have something to do with the paperwork you had to fill out?"

"Regrettably."

My cheeks started buzzing like I'd been slapped in the face. "No. He didn't."

"Against my advice to the contrary, he did."

A ringing in my ears joined the chaos. "He can't."

"Trust me, I don't like it any more than you do."

A dozen violent feelings fought for dominance, but disbelief was winning. "To whom?"

Nic rolled his eyes. "Who do you think?"

"Cea!" I dropped the shopping bag and grabbed both sides of my face. Of course, it was Cea. Ephesus had been sweet on Nic's sister for a while, but I had no idea they were thinking of getting *married.*

Nic stooped to grab a protein bar that had tumbled to the floor. "Eyup. Welcome to the family, sis. Thanks to that tax form I just turned in, we're now legally related in more than one way, so that's weird."

"Weird" didn't even begin to describe it. "But—why? How?"

"I called the base as soon as I landed. I caught him proposing, and instead of being embarrassed like normal people, they asked me to marry them."

"And you said *yes?*"

Nic gestured with the protein bar, almost smacking the rider next to him. "I couldn't say no! She's my sister!"

"Never stopped you before." Oddly, I felt more betrayed by Nic than anyone else; surely, he was on my side with this one.

"Fair point, but only a fool messes with a woman's wedding."

I yelled as anger suddenly overtook my other emotions. "I can't believe him! Sorry," I added when the person on the bench next to me gave me a terrified look. She decided she'd rather ride elsewhere and got up. Nic quickly took her spot.

I slumped back against the window as the reality of my new family tree sank into me. My own brother got married—*without me*. "I can't believe he would do this to me," I repeated, this time at an appropriate decibel.

"Honestly, same," Nic agreed.

"He's my only sibling! He's literally the only close family I have left. And he didn't even tell me he was going to propose." I wanted to be happy for them, I really did. I loved both of them, and they deserved happiness—especially my brother, after all he'd been through. But to get married on a whim and not even mention it to me? That was adding insult to injury when I was already approaching crush depth with anxiety and stress.

I tried to release my frustration and just ended up making a weird growling sound. "I'm going to kill him when we get back."

It was an exaggeration, but Nic was on board with the plan. "I'll hold, you punch."

I couldn't help but laugh. My anger melted as I realized the absurdity of the whole situation. "Well, I guess I could start telling people you're my brother, if you like that better."

He turned to me with a gaze so dead that his face might as well have been stone. "I don't."

I smirked.

We spent the rest of the ride in relative silence. Nic scrolled through an offline map on his phone, searching for bus routes. I kept my mind busy by praying for Ephesus and Cea and watching the TV that was mounted at the top of the wall. Some talk show was playing. The subtitles were in simplified Chinese, but I enjoyed trying to guess what they were saying based on their hand gestures and facial expressions.

And then the news came on.

It was a replay of last night's gala. I stiffened as I recognized the palace, the guests—and General Secretary Mong. He smiled benevolently as he gave a gracious bow to the camera.

"Nic," I hissed, poking him.

He looked up. His face folded in a frown as the screen flashed to clips of the various celebrities and political giants that had been in attendance. There were several staged shots as Mong and foreign diplomats posed for the camera, faking smiles and embracing each other as if a good photo could prove that all was well with the world.

Suddenly, I appeared.

I sucked in my breath as my own face filled the screen. My dress glittered in the flash of a thousand camera bulbs as I lifted my skirts and bowed. I was surprised at how smooth and elegant the motion looked; my face was calm, like I had rehearsed this moment a thousand times. The camera was zoomed in too far to see the reaction of the crowd; was that by accident or design? Nevertheless, the pleasure on the General's face was evident as he returned the gesture.

Some Mandarin characters flashed across the screen, and then the clip was gone as quickly as it had appeared. "What did it say?" I whispered to Nic.

He shook his head—although whether that was because he couldn't read it or because he didn't want to tell me, I'll never know. "Keep your head down," he hissed.

I glanced around the subway car, but no one was paying us any mind. Hopefully, without my manicured makeup, extra curls, and sparkling dress, I wouldn't attract attention. But I still tucked my bleached hair behind my ear as I sank into the seat.

It took over two hours for us to reach the end of the line. I fought to keep up with Nic as he shoved his way through the mid-afternoon shopping crowd to the nearest bus stop. The shelter roof was modeled after a traditional tile design, and the stained concrete walls had been retrofitted with a chaotic array of digital signboards. Nic planted himself in front of one and studied the scrolling text. After a minute, he started tugging on his mustache.

I knew what that meant. He had no idea where to go.

I sat down on a nearby bench and started praying, hard. There had to be another solution besides fleeing to the mountains. Weren't there safe houses, black markets, places outside the law? There were almost thirty million people in this province; we couldn't be the only criminals on the run. Surely there were people willing to do things under the radar for the right price—like Andes, the technician and tattoo artist I used back in Boston.

The question was how to find people outside the law. I'd needed a referral to get to Andes, and I didn't know anyone here. Would Nic know someone? He had obviously spent time in Beijing in the past; he had dated Asia of all people. But that had been years ago; all of his contacts may have gone cold.

My eyes wandered around the shelter, searching for answers—and that's when I saw it.

It was small and disfigured; the resemblance was so crude that you wouldn't know what it was unless you were already looking for it. I stood and walked over for a closer look. It was drawn on the underside of the roof near the corner. It was nearly lost amongst the collage of other graffiti and coarse sayings that had been added by rebellious teens over the years. But I knew what it was.

A thunderbird.

9: NIC

"Nic," Phil hissed.

Her clammy fingers brushed my arm. I grimaced and shrugged her off. Physical contact wasn't my favorite thing, and she'd reached for me with her right hand—the hand that still contained an active bomb. Supposedly, it would only detonate for its intended target, but I didn't particularly trust Jayde's programming skills. Until we could get the wires in her hand removed, I'd just as soon avoid getting all touchy-feely.

"What?" I sighed and glanced back at her.

"Look." She attempted to subtly point at the roof of the bus stop. Almost nothing Phil did was subtle; it looked like she was having a seizure as she jerked her head and rolled her eyes upward.

I followed her gaze, saw what it was, and immediately knew we had to leave.

"Let's go." I shouldered my backpack and spun on my heels.

She did the exact opposite, planting herself in front of the signboard in a way that looked anything but nonchalant. "No, wait, I think this can help us. What do the characters say?"

There were a handful of simplified Chinese characters scribbled next to the thunderbird; I could tell they had been added at the same time due to the fading of the ink. They were numbers—a bus route, probably. All the more reason we should get far away from this stop.

"We need to get out of here." I made a second attempt to leave.

"Nic, wait!"

I did no such thing. I shoved past a group of commuters and hurried down the street, knowing she'd keep up out of fear of being left behind.

It took her a block to catch up. "Nic, stop, please!"

"We're not safe here." I turned into an alley, eager to get out of sight.

She found a burst of energy and darted ahead of me. She halted and attempted to block the way. "But what if we are? What if—what if that's the solution?"

I knew exactly what she was suggesting, and it was a terrible idea. "Absolutely not—"

"No, don't you see?" she blathered on. "There's an underground here, and they know me. If we can find a safe house or a point of contact and tell them I'm here, they'll take care of us."

The Chinese underground was the last thing she should be getting involved with. "No," I repeated, louder, hoping the volume would get her attention. "We're going to get out of the city and call your brother."

My attempt to regain control of the situation backfired; she just raised her volume to match mine. "But what can he do? Surely Asia's watching the activity on base. We need temp files— and the underground can get us those."

"That would be great, if it weren't for two inconvenient complications." I spelled it out for her, even though she really should have been smart enough to see how foolish her plan was. "If we waltz in there and announce ourselves, not only will they know we're in Beijing, but they'll also know what our temporary identities are. Both of those are pieces of information I'd like to keep to ourselves."

"No, Nic, you don't understand," she cried, even though I definitely did. "It's not like that. I'm Blue Fire."

The very sound of the forbidden callsign made my blood run cold. *No, you're not,* I thought. *You're just a dumb teenage girl, and you have no idea who you're dealing with.*

She mistook my silence as consent. "They trust me—I'm their leader. If we tell them I'm here, they can help us."

I was sure they would—and then we'd be right back where we started, with Philadelphia in the middle of a war she didn't understand. "Enough," I demanded, and shoved her out of the way. "I've made up my mind."

She stumbled and almost fell over. "No, Nic, just listen to me, please!" She regained her balance and grabbed my jacket sleeve. "You have to trust me! I can do this—I can fix this!"

Her pitiful statement pierced a memory, and I snapped. "No, you can't!"

My shout ricocheted off the dumpster beside us, finally silencing her. She let go of my sleeve. I took a deep breath and lowered my voice, but only for the benefit of any eavesdroppers.

"No, you can't fix this, *Andromeda,*" I slurred the name into a warning, "and you know why?"

She did—we both did—but I stated it for the court anyway.

"Because you got us into this mess. We're stranded in Beijing without any way to get online, hunted by the worst woman in history, because you thought you were a hero. You got mixed up with people and politics you didn't understand, and you almost started a war and got us all killed."

My anger wavered, but not because there wasn't plenty of it to go around. No, I abruptly realized that it wasn't her ignorance that bothered me. It wasn't the fact that she'd gotten tangled up in a petty revolution that made me so furious.

It was the fact that I'd tried, again and again, to reason with her. And yet, after all I'd done for her, she still wasn't listening.

I was done bargaining with her. I hadn't come all the way back to Earth and risked my life to save her just to have her throw it all away. I was going to get us off this planet alive if it was the last thing I did, and if that meant I had to play the bad guy for a while, so be it.

"Look, I came back for you because, believe it or not, I don't want you dead. But I'm sick and tired of having my decisions questioned after all I've done to try to help you." I kept my back to her as I continued. "So from now on, you will let me be the adult. We're going out of the city so I can find someone who can help us get online. You will let me do the talking, and I don't want to hear another word about the underground. Have I made myself clear?"

She was silent. I turned and looked back at her.

Her eyes were on the ground as she gripped her chest with both arms. "Yessir," she mumbled, and I heard in her voice the shake that told me the argument was over.

"Good," I said with palpable relief, even though I wondered how long our impasse would last. "Now come on."

I led the way down the alley in the opposite direction of the bus stop—even though I knew that was neurotic. Just because the underground was using the bus didn't mean we couldn't. They didn't know Phil was in Beijing, and even if they did, they likely wouldn't recognize her with her blue contacts and bleached hair.

But by the time I admitted to myself that I was overreacting, we'd already walked a mile in the wrong direction. Although "wrong" was a relative term when I didn't really know where we were going. I knew I wanted to get out of the city, into the country where the surveillance was hopefully lighter, but that was easier said than done when the free public transportation system only went so far.

Still, I would rather spend the night in a village than the sewers of the inner city, so I took us to another bus stop and doubled back to where we came from, hoping Phil wouldn't question it. By then, rush hour had started, so we waited in line for over an hour before we caught a bus out of town.

And that's about when I realized I was in deep trouble. Phil wasn't talking. At all.

In fact, she didn't say a word the entire trip. Several times, I glanced back to make sure I hadn't lost her. She stayed close and didn't complain, but she didn't once turn to look up at me.

We finally managed to squeeze onto a bus, although it was standing room only. We rode the line as far as it would take us, out into the suburbs of Beijing. Of course, given the intensity of China's urban sprawl, "suburb" was a bit of a loose term. The area we found ourselves in was almost as densely packed as the inner city. The only difference was that everything was newer and more orderly, to the point of being bland. Endless rows of apartments were laid out in perfect squares like prison cells. A deliberate attempt had been made to leave room for grass in between the buildings, but it did little to soften the severity of concrete and tile.

By then it was nearly dark, and Phil still wasn't talking. I was contemplating doing the unthinkable and initiating conversation when I got a cruel reminder that we weren't alone in the universe.

It started to rain.

I sensed the shift in the wind and knew we only had minutes before it turned into a downpour. We were still in the shopping district where the bus had let us off, so I figured our best bet was to find shelter in an alley. I led us behind the buildings and ran until I found an abandoned corner void of any prying eyes.

The strip of shops had been closed down, making me hope the apartments above were empty as well. I climbed the metal staircase and peeked through the iron grates into the grimy windows; everything was dark and uninhabited. I tried the doors, but they were all locked. I contemplated kicking one down, but there was still power going to the building, which meant the alarm system could be online. By now the rain was coming down in torrents, so I decided not to press our luck and accept the relative shelter of the awning.

We set up camp in the middle of the building, shielded from the wind by some forgotten boxes. The air was still damp and chilly, but at least the concrete was dry. I divvied up our dinner, then stared at the contents of the bag and appreciated the severity of our situation. We could stretch the food for a few more days if needed, but the water would run out tomorrow. Unless I could find a sanitary place to refill our bottles, I'd have to send Phil to buy more—and then we would start all over with our deadly game of hide-and-seek with Asia.

Before I could work out a solution to that problem, our solitude was rudely interrupted. A crash came from the far end of the building, loud enough to be heard over the rain pounding on the concrete. I dropped the bag and whipped around, but there was nothing to see. There were no lights in the alley except the streetlamp at the end of the block, and the only movement was the water pouring off the gutter.

Phil sat up straight. "I'll go check," I assured her, even though she hadn't said anything.

I crept to the end of the building. As I neared the last apartment, I heard it again. This time, it was more of a scratch and a rustle, and it was clearly coming from the pile of boards and trash that was heaped on the edge of the balcony.

I really hope there's not a homeless person under here, I thought to myself, then grabbed the topmost board and flung it aside.

It wasn't a person. It was a cat.

It was a scrawny, pathetic little thing. It huddled against the building, mewing pitifully and staring up at me with yellow eyes that were too big for its stunted body. Its dark gray fur was sopping wet, and its eyes were crusted almost shut with gunk. The stupid animal looked like it had already expended eight of its lives, and I wondered if it would survive the night.

Suddenly, Phil found her voice. "Kitty!"

I sighed loudly in relief. She gave me a funny look.

"Never mind," I said. "And no, you can't keep it."

"But why not?" She walked over and knelt beside me. She held out her hand and clucked encouragingly. The cat answered the summons. It got up—and came straight to me.

I jerked back as it tried to wrap itself around my ankle. "Because it'll do stuff like *that*. Also, it might belong to somebody."

Phil pried the cat off my pant leg and cuddled it in her arms. "I doubt he has an owner. Look at him."

She was probably right. If the poor animal did have owners, they weren't feeding him. But that didn't mean *I* was going to pick up the slack. "And what exactly are *you* going to feed him? He can't eat trail mix, even if I was willing to share."

She scratched him behind the ears. He accepted the attention and settled in her arms, even though he kept his fat eyes on me. "I don't have to feed him—he'll eat mice or whatever."

"Well, he might starve for lack of ambition," I commented, noting how skinny he was.

Phil was not deterred in the slightest. She skipped back over to our backpacks and unclipped the blanket. She sat cross-legged on the floor, made a nest with the blanket, and tucked the cat in her lap. He immediately started purring like he was king of the universe.

"I'm going to name him Tommy," she announced.

"Why, because it's a tom cat?" I snarked.

She wrinkled her nose at me. "No, after my dad."

I heard the clip in her voice and saw the flicker in her eyes—grief over the loss of a parent. I knew that grief all too well.

And that's when I remembered that Phil had suffered through her own special kind of purgatory since coming back to Earth. She'd been punished enough for her mistakes; she really didn't need me to yell at her.

I sat down next to her, leaning against the building and folding my long legs to keep them out of the rain. "Look... I'm sorry I yelled at you."

I expected her to perk up, like she usually did any time I was a decent human being. But she didn't. Instead, she looked down and turned red with shame. "No, you're right," she mumbled. "I never should have become a Nolan."

It was an abrupt declaration that, as far as I was concerned, had nothing to do with what we'd been discussing earlier. "I'm going to need more context, because I wasn't privy to the five hours of internal monologue that led up to that statement."

I meant it as a joke and an invitation. I failed at both objectives.

"I was never supposed to be a Nolan," she repeated, which literally gave me no additional information.

"Explain," I prodded.

Instead of answering, she started petting the cat more aggressively. He didn't appreciate her anxious hand movements and opened one eye to squint at me, as if expecting me to commiserate.

"Philadelphia." I elbowed her to get her to stop. "Talk to me."

"I'm not supposed to be here!" she shrieked. Tears filled her eyes at the same time a rare emotion made it onto her face: anger. "I never should have met the General, I never should have come to Beijing, I never should have agreed to be Blue Fire, I never should have come back to Earth, I never should have a recorded any videos, and I never should have taken the Nolans' name."

That was a whole lot of conjecture—and at least one of those statements was empirically false.

Tears were winning the battle for her emotions. She scooped the stupid cat up and buried her face in his neck, sobbing into his already-wet fur. "You were right, you were right about everything. I'm not a hero, I'm not Blue Fire, and I'm not Andromeda Nolan. I should have just stayed Philadelphia Smyrna."

"I never said that," I argued, and as soon as the words left my mouth, I knew.

She *was* supposed to be Andromeda Nolan. She was supposed to go back to Earth, record videos, and lead the revolution. She was Blue Fire. She was supposed to be here, in Beijing. And she absolutely was supposed to meet the General.

She just wasn't supposed to kill him.

I saw it all, clear as day, as if it were a reality that had already happened. The details were sharp and precise, and the picture felt almost more real than the damp alley in front of me. It had been years since I'd had a vision like that, but I knew what it was and where it came from.

And I wanted absolutely nothing to do with it.

I didn't want to live in that world: a world where Philadelphia truly was a Nolan. A reality where she lived amongst the elites in Beijing and played politics with her wealth and influence. That was the life I'd had ten years ago.

I didn't want to go back to that life. And I didn't want that life for her, either.

Phil, thankfully, saw none of that for herself. She just sat there, sniveling into that stupid cat, crushed under the weight of her teenage failures. I knew that if I didn't get her out of the pit, she'd spend all night crying.

"Hey."

She didn't look up at me, but I waited until her breathing had slowed before continuing.

"I promise I'll get us out of this. I will get us home, and you won't have to worry about any of that ever again. Okay?"

"Okay," she repeated. She gave an ugly sniff and lifted her head, mercifully allowing the cat to breathe again. He gave a disgruntled mew but didn't seem motivated enough to vacate his warm nest in the blankets.

With her emotional crisis averted, my mind immediately went back to processing bigger problems. I needed some peace and quiet, but that meant I had to distract her. "Here." I reached into my backpack and fished out the pair of earbuds Narissa had given us. I tossed them at Phil. "I downloaded part of my music archive to the phone."

Something close to a smile warmed her face; she knew what I meant. She put the earbuds in and pulled the phone out of her backpack. She scrolled through the menus until she found one of the old worship albums I had downloaded for just such an emergency. She leaned against the wall and pulled her knees to her chest, stroking the cat's fur. The stupid animal accepted his fate and started purring.

I waited until Phil had zoned out and closed her eyes before getting up and moving to the end of the balcony. I sat on the top step, careful to stay under the protection of the awning, and tented my arms on my knees. I stared out at the pouring rain and tried to rouse my inner genius.

We needed new files—especially Phil. That was apparent to me now. Andromeda Nolan had become just as much of a curse as Philadelphia Smyrna, and if she had any hope of avoiding the underground—let alone Asia—she needed to become a new person. I didn't relish the idea of walking her through another identity crisis, but it was necessary.

Unfortunately, clean files were not easy to come by. Andes could do it, but going to him was too risky; both Jayde and Asia knew about him. Besides, we needed clean files before we were going to be able to get out of the country. That meant we needed a contact in China, someone who could launder money so effectively that even Asia wouldn't be able to find the electronic trail.

And there was only one person I'd heard of who could do that. If she was even a real person.

I groaned and raked my hand over my untrimmed beard. I didn't like it one bit, especially since it involved admitting to Phil that I changed my mind, but we were running out of options.

If it would keep Phil safe, this was a risk I was going to have to take.

10: PHILADELPHIA

The sun was high overhead when I awoke the next morning. It took a full minute of me squinting at the bright ball of gas before I processed what that meant.

I'd overslept.

I jerked upright, fighting to get out of the blanket. My cat squealed as I accidentally dumped him on the concrete. "Nic!"

"Good morning, princess," he chirped from where he sat on the top step. "Someone slept well."

I paused to assess my five senses and realized he was right—it had been a good night's sleep. My joints were stiff from sleeping on concrete for the second night in a row, but my head felt clear. How I had been able to sleep so well on the street in the rain was beyond me; I could only imagine the worship music had played a factor.

I removed the earbuds and tucked them in the pocket of Nic's backpack. "Why didn't you wake me up?"

"I figured you needed the sleep." He chucked a protein bar at me.

I was in no frame of mind to catch it, so it plunked off my shoulder and fell on the ground. Tommy pounced on it and began clawing at the shiny plastic. "Yeah, but I thought we had to 'keep moving.'"

The glare he shot me over his shoulder told me I'd better watch my attitude. "We do, but I'm in absolutely no rush to get where we're going. Besides, service doesn't start until five."

"Service?"

He took a deep breath. "We're going to find Jael."

My universe stopped and rebooted when I realized what that meant. "Really? Why? How?"

He groaned and closed his eyes, as if he were already regretting his decision. "Which question do you want an answer to? Because I only have the mental capacity for one."

I paused to consider that. I really wanted to know why—what had happened overnight to convince him to change his mind? Was it something I said? Did he finally agree with me? I didn't even need a replay of his whole thought process; I really just wanted an apology.

But I didn't need one.

After pausing to cast a prayer up at God, I turned back to Nic. "Let's go with 'how.'"

"If Narissa is telling the truth, then it sounds like most of the Christians around here know who she is. Our best bet is to find a church and ask them to refer us."

Now that was a plan I could get behind—except I had absolutely no idea how to find a church in Beijing. Christianity had been illegal here even longer than it had been in America. Narissa might know of a congregation, but it wasn't safe to contact her.

I looked up at Nic. "I don't suppose *you* know of any churches," I deadpanned.

"Unless they've all been rounded up and executed, there's a group that used to meet every night in a factory on the river," he declared without batting an eyelash.

"Wait, *what*?"

He ignored my implied disbelief. "But it's all the way on the south side of the province, so we've got some walking to do." He stood and stretched. "Rise and shine, sleeping beauty. It's time to move. And don't you dare bring that cat."

I had so many questions, but Nic seemed determined to avoid them. After we argued for several minutes about my cat, he hustled me down to the square. Tommy followed of his own accord, making the whole argument moot.

Nic sent me into the nearest store to buy more food and water. We were about to head to the other side of the province; we might as well make a mark online and send Asia in the opposite direction. I refilled our bag, picked up a battery pack for the phone and some canned food for Tommy, and ordered two large coffees. I paid without issue; the clerk barely even made eye contact.

I stole a glance at the messaging app as I hurried back to Nic. It was still signed in under his username, so most of the unread messages were from people I didn't know. But I did recognize the top two users. Ephesus had sent a "thank you," followed by:

PLEASE TELL BLUE FIRE TO CALL ME AS SOON AS YOU CAN SAFELY GET ONLINE

I swallowed a nip of guilt and switched over to the chat with Stanyard. In his usual fashion, he'd sent a message every few hours. Most of them were reminders that he was praying for me, but the most recent message was less encouraging:

FYI, GREEN DRAGON HAS NOT CHECKED IN. NO ONE KNOWS WHERE HE IS. BE CAREFUL

I paused on the sidewalk outside of the store and worked my jaw. That meant one of two things: Either Jayde had gotten arrested at the party, or he had escaped and was still in Beijing. Seeing as there was no mention of an arrest on the news—or, apparently, on Jayde's file—I had a sinking feeling it was the latter.

I clicked in the box and prepared to send Stanyard a quick message, but before I could figure out what to say, a text came through.

It was from Asia.

YOU MUST BE SO TIRED AND HUNGRY

I froze. She knew I was online; she must have been watching my file and saw the purchase.

YOU DON'T HAVE TO DO THIS. YOU KNOW I WON'T HURT YOU.

Do I know that? I wondered. She sent one final plea.

JUST COME HOME. I'M WORRIED ABOUT YOU.

I quickly took the phone offline and hid it in my backpack.

I joined up with Nic where he waited on a nearby bench. He was trying and failing to keep Tommy out of his lap. Knowing we'd get complaints if I took a cat on the bus, I convinced Tommy to climb in my backpack; he was so scrawny that he fit even with the Bible and other objects stashed in there.

With my new pet safely hidden, we ran to the closest bus stop. It was midday, and the lines weren't long. We were able to fit on the next bus. We rode it across the neighborhood to the subway line that would carry us south.

I daren't talk about an illegal religion while we were crammed in a train with dozens of other people, so I let Nic savor his coffee in silence. We cut across the province, then jumped on another bus that took us deep into the heart of a riverside district.

The neighborhood was old, but not in the smoggy, over-processed way of the inner city. As I watched out the window at the passing streets, it was like time was getting stripped away in layers, revealing the ancient civilization that had once thrived in this valley. The skyrises faded into the background, replaced by narrow two- and three-story homes that crowded the riverbank.

Their foundations dipped into the canal, and stains on their white-washed walls revealed the height of past floods. Willows crowded for space in between the houses, their lacy leaves dragging in the water, and red-and-gold lanterns dangled from the gray roofs. The whole town was peaceful and strangely quiet, as if time moved as slowly as the ripples on the water.

The bus let us off on a street corner. We crossed a bridge to the other side of the river, and I paused in the middle and appreciated the view of the sunlight warming the greenish water. "It's beautiful," I commented, and turned to Nic for confirmation.

He barely gave it a passing glance. "Come on."

We found a secluded park and stopped under the shade of a mulberry tree to eat. I let Tommy out of my backpack and gave him a can of food, which he licked clean.

Meanwhile, I tried to muster up the courage to consume another protein bar. After two days of wandering, the sugary packaged food wasn't cutting it. As much as I hated to admit it, Asia was right; I *was* tired and hungry. If I didn't have any sense, it would be tempting to go back to the Nolan estate.

I told Nic about the text messages. He grunted and crushed his empty water bottle. "Hopefully this Jael character can get us temporary files—or has access to a secured line. We're not going anywhere until we can get online without Asia knowing."

I reached down to stroke Tommy's back and weighed my words carefully. "So... how *do* you know about this church, anyway?"

Nic didn't fall for it. "I told you that you only got to ask one question, and you've expended that credit for the day."

Unfortunately for him, I was feeling equally stubborn. "You know I'm just going to keep bugging you until you answer me, right?"

He grumbled, but it was the kind of grumble that told me I was about to get my way. "It's not rocket science," he said without looking at me. "You've met my parents."

"Yeah, and I've also met you."

He turned to stare at me, making me wonder if my comment had cut deeper than intended.

He shifted his attention back to the uneven brick road. "My dad used to come to Beijing for business once or twice a year. The factory owner is—was—a partner of his. Dad encouraged him to let people meet in his building. In exchange, Dad granted him an exclusive contract to produce a patented part for his science stations."

"He bribed him," I clarified.

Nic blinked, as if he'd never thought of it that way. "I guess so."

I chewed the last bite of my protein bar as this information cast new light on the gentle, innocent man I'd met back in Boston. I knew Mr. Von had been another person before the neurosurgery, but this story painted an entirely different picture than the one I'd been imagining. This Mr. Von was intelligent, powerful, cunning—not unlike his son.

It also made me think of the massive bank account I had sitting at home. For the first time, I wondered if there was more I should be doing with my money.

Nic continued his story before I could fully process the thought. "When I was a teenager, he used to bring me along on his trips whenever he could, so I've been there several times. If they're still meeting at the factory, hopefully they'll remember Dad's name and let us in."

"And if they're not still meeting there?"

"Then we're no worse off than we started—and maybe they know where another meeting place is." Nic shrugged, but I could tell the gesture was forced. His voice was so artificially calm that it sounded robotic. "They were still meeting there when I came back in college."

I tried to pinpoint where that fit in the timeline of Nic's life. "What happened?"

"What do you mean?" he returned, but his eyes were avoiding mine.

I leaned forward, trying to get in his line of vision. "Nic, I'm not stupid."

"I didn't say you were."

He actually had—several times—but that was beside the point. "I can do basic math. If you went to church in college, that means you were going without your dad. Which kind of implies you wanted to go."

He swiveled to face me. "What is it you want, Phil? What do you want me to say?"

Tact was getting me nowhere, so I decided to come right out with it. "I want to know why you're not a Christian anymore."

He drew back from me, putting as much distance between us as he could without getting up and walking away. "If you're looking for a Judas Iscariot moment so you can make my tragic backstory fit in your tidy little sense of morality, then you're not going to find it. Stop trying to justify me."

"I'm not," I snapped, because that truly *wasn't* what I wanted. It didn't have to make sense, and I certainly didn't have to agree. I just wanted to understand.

"Then why do you care?" he challenged.

"Because I care about you."

The words slipped out before I could filter them, but I didn't take them back. They were true.

The anger evaporated from his face, leaving a void in his expression. I took advantage of his silence and forged ahead. "Look, I know this concept makes you want to throw up or whatever, but I care about you. You saved my life at the party. And before that, you tried to help me with my dad. You even 'adopted' me. For these past few months, you've... you've been there for me."

As I rambled on, my voice began to shake. Not because I was nervous, but because I was terrified of how true my words really were. Ever since Rott, Nic *had* cared about me—in his own sarcastic, socially inept way. To the best of his ability, he was trying to protect me.

And I owed him an apology.

He grimaced and looked royally uncomfortable. "Phil, look—"

I put up my hand and cut him off. I wasn't going to let him avoid the conversation, not this time. "No, just listen. I need you to hear this. I need you to know that I'm sorry. For what I said on the phone."

I flinched as the memories of that heated, hurtful conversation echoed in my ears. I swallowed and forced as much intention into my voice as I could, struggling to rebuild the wall I'd torn down with my words.

"I don't think you're a coward. I think you're brave, and I know you risked your reputation and the base when you agreed to become my legal guardian. Let alone when you came back to Earth to save me."

Tommy wrapped himself around Nic's ankles, as if agreeing with my assessment of his character. Nic shoved him away. "Philadelphia—"

"Just listen, please," I begged. "I know you care about me. And… it was wrong of me to say that you don't understand what it's like to be unassimilated. I see that now. With everything you told me about Asia and your parents… You do understand."

As soon as the words left my mouth, I realized I'd answered my own question. *That's* what had happened: Asia. Asia was the wedge that had come between Nic and the Lord. I tried to imagine what he must have felt. He had done what he thought was right—made the courageous choice to delete Red Rain—only to have the woman he loved kill his parents in retaliation. If that had happened to me, I would have questioned my ethics, too.

Or maybe that wasn't what happened. Maybe I was completely wrong about him.

Maybe… it didn't matter.

I looked up at him. He'd gone eerily silent. He was still staring at me, his eyebrows twisted in a gesture I didn't have a translation for.

I had no idea how to end this awkward conversation I'd started, so I settled for repeating myself. "I just… want you to know I'm sorry. I apologize for the things I said, and I don't think of you like that."

He looked down at my cat, who was attacking a fallen leaf. "I know you don't," he said after a minute, and I realized, in retrospect, that was the best reaction I could have hoped for in the situation.

We waited in the park until it was nearly five o'clock, then walked the rest of the way to the factory. It was situated on the outskirts of town, where the river widened and picked up enough energy to power the industry. The building had aged a little less gracefully than the town; its pipes and smokestacks were bleeding rust, and the windows were clouded, with many boarded over. But the factory was still in full operation, with steam chugging into the sky and the omnipresent grind of machinery filling the air, which I hoped was a good sign.

Nic explained that service happened at five o'clock, with shift change concealing the flow of people in and out of the building. The dock gates were open, and a stream of people converged towards the security checkpoint like a dammed river. Most of them wore the blue uniforms and white hardhats of factory workers, but I caught a few civilians and office staff mixed in, their coats pulled up and their hats pulled down to conceal their faces. I hid Tommy in my backpack and stayed close to Nic.

He waited until the crowd had dwindled and then joined the back of the line. We were almost the last ones to approach the gate.

An exhausted teenager who looked far too young to have a job like this squinted at us through the glass of the security booth. "Name?"

"Von Nieuwenhuyse," Nic said, enunciating carefully.

I couldn't see the kid's expression behind the face mask he wore, but I could see the twitch of his bushy eyebrows. He looked down at his desk. He pushed his tablet aside, revealing a water-stained ledger that was nearly buried under the other paraphernalia on the desk. I could see the list held a mix of Mandarin and English surnames.

The teen scanned the paper with his finger. "I don't see you on tonight's shift," he said, English poor but translatable.

"Maybe you don't understand me." Nic leaned closer to the speaker in the glass. "I said Von Nieuwenhuyse, as in Dr. Paul Von Nieuwenhuyse."

I held my breath while the kid recalibrated, and then his eyes lit up. He tapped his tablet, and the keypad on the outside of the security booth lit up. "Fingerprints, please," he instructed.

My heart stopped. *No, God, no.*

Nic took a step back, and the teenager misinterpreted his hesitation. "For internal records only," he assured. "You understand."

I did understand—except that Nic's fingerprint would set off a security warning and alert everyone that he was wanted criminal, internal system or not.

"He's with me," I volunteered, and shoved my way forward. I pressed my thumb to the keypad before Nic could stop me.

The screen chirped, and the teenager nodded. "You're good. Now you, please, sir."

Nic put his hands up. "Look, I really just need to speak to your manager. It won't take long. He's a friend of my father's."

The teen finally picked up on the fact that something was wrong. I saw the shift in his posture—the straightening of his back, the narrowing of his eyes. "I'm sorry, sir, but I can't do that."

"It's important," Nic insisted, and even I could tell that he was getting desperate. "You don't understand—my father sent me."

"I'm sorry, sir," the kid repeated. He slid his hand beneath the desk. "But I don't know you."

I saw what he was reaching for—a panic button—and knew I had to do something before we caused a scene.

"Then tell him *I* want to see him," I declared, putting myself in front of Nic.

The teen hesitated, his finger over the button. "And who are you?"

"Andromeda—" Nic threatened, reaching for me.

I shrugged out of his grasp and glanced around to make sure no one was watching. I knew what I was about to do was dangerous, but we didn't have a choice. We had to get in and see Jael. She was our only hope.

I faced the kid and rolled up my right sleeve, revealing my thunderbird tattoo. "I am Blue Fire."

11: NIC

The ticket boy squinted at Phil like he didn't believe her, and for a desperate second, I prayed that he wouldn't.

But before I could regain control of the situation, Phil reached up and popped her blue contacts out, revealing her natural brown eyes. The kid uttered an oath in Mandarin.

I copied him, swearing loudly in English and hoping everyone, especially Phil, heard.

The kid yanked his face mask off and threw it on the counter. "Hurry—this way."

I was just about to grab Phil's arm and pull her in the opposite direction when the kid punched a button on the wall of the control booth. I heard the squeak and groan of tired hinges and turned to see the massive dock gates closing.

I swore again, not that anyone was deterred by my objections.

The kid scrambled out of the control booth and took off across the yard at a run, waving at us to follow. He shouted in Mandarin at the guards loitering around the lot. His words were too urgent for me to translate, but I understood the gist when the guards fell into step beside us, weapons ready.

Phil, for once in her life, seemed wholly unafraid.

The kid led us around the back of the factory to a shipping entrance. The garage door stood open, as if they'd been waiting to receive us this entire time. The grind of the factory was unfiltered now, made worse by the dissonant chatter of workers. We ran up the dock and past the endless rows of lockers, where a few straggling employees were suiting up.

I tried to grab Phil's shoulder and hold her back. "What in the world are you—"

I stopped when I saw one of the guards glance at me. I read the frown on his face and saw his finger slide into position on the trigger and knew I'd better not try anything here.

We followed the kid up a flight of stairs and across a catwalk that overlooked the production floor. Rows of blindingly lit workstations lined the cavernous concrete room. Several hundred gloved workers labored in tandem with bright yellow robotic arms, manipulating trays of circuitry. I was extremely familiar with the blueprint for the machinery and could tell that it had changed little in the last decade; clearly, the factory was still producing the coveted part for interstellar space stations.

I swallowed an irrational burst of rage. Apparently, Tang, the factory owner, had fared better than my father.

We descended in an elevator to the basement, where the mess hall was located. I struggled to stay in control of my faculties as unwelcome muscle memory kicked in. I remembered everything. The slight jerk as the rusty elevator hit the bottom. The smell of bland, over-processed food and hot plastic. And the moan of collective prayer in several languages, one of which I wish I didn't understand.

The elevator doors ground open, revealing a service in full swing. The stuffy, fluorescent-lit hall was packed, even more so than it would be during lunch hour. People of all ages and races crowded the aisles in between the yellowed plastic tables, while parents balanced their little children on the pea-green chairs so they could get a better view. I noted that attendance had at least doubled, if not tripled, since the last time I visited. I would have expected the opposite trend.

At the far end of the hall, on the podium normally used for announcements, a couple of pastors paced back and forth, reading from contraband Bibles while they joined the throng in prayer. I scanned the crowd for familiar faces, searching for anyone I even remotely trusted, but saw no one.

A few guards stood watch inside the entrance. The ticket boy grabbed one of them and whispered in his ear. The soldier snapped to attention and turned to Phil. After a moment of regarding her in wonder, he saluted. His partners copied the gesture.

I felt my blood boil at the same time my skin went cold with fear.

One of the guards gestured for Phil to follow him. Before I could object, she stepped forward, and he led her away. I quickly lost sight of her as they wove through the congested crowd. I sensed the shift in the atmosphere—the worship tapering off as people took notice of the stranger and began to whisper. I felt eyes looking in my direction and backed up, but the guards blocked the hall to the elevator.

Suddenly, Phil appeared on the podium at the opposite end of the room. The guard bent and spoke to her, and she obliged, taking off her backpack and rolling up her right sleeve.

"Phil, don't!" I yelled, not realizing until too late that I'd spoken aloud. Several people turned to me, but I was quickly forgotten when one of the pastors took a mic and called for attention.

As if Jesus had just commanded the storm to cease, the whole room stilled. In the brief second of silence, I tried to catch Phil's gaze.

Don't do this!

She didn't see me. The pastor cupped the microphone and announced something in Mandarin. A murmur washed over the crowd, punctuated by several shrieks of surprise.

Phil frowned at the pastor, not understanding. He grinned and repeated himself in English.

"Blue Fire has returned!"

Then he stepped aside, leaving her center stage, her tattoo bared for all the world to see.

The crowd devolved into a tornado of cheers, claps, and stomps. The guards on the sidelines shouted military slogans and saluted. A small child near me started jumping up and down on the table and squealing about the "thunderbird," at the encouragement of her older siblings.

Phil stared at the crowd, petrified. For one final moment, she was the scared, pitiful teenage girl I thought I knew.

And then she smiled.

The pastor handed her the microphone. She took it and strode to the edge of the podium like she had been preparing for this moment her entire life. The crowd hushed unbidden, a few excited whispers escaping as they waited, no doubt expecting some great speech.

I was horrified when she opened her mouth and gave them one.

"God is for you."

The words were quiet, hesitant, as if she were testing the ice with them. She let them hang there while she frowned in thought, no doubt giving the voice in her head time to catch up. When she spoke again, I could tell the words were not her own.

"He sees you. He knows your faithfulness. He knows how much you have risked to be here, and He wants you to know that He is *for* you. And greater is He that is in us than he that is the world!"

Her volume skyrocketed, just in time to avoid getting drowned out by the applause and cheers of *Amen!* that erupted. She rattled on without waiting for them to quiet down.

"Because *His* is the name that's above every other name, every government, every spirit, every demonic force. He is above the United, above communism, above socialism, above war—and He will *always* be victorious!"

Such grand words from a little girl who had no strength or power to back them up, and the people were delirious over them. She leaned out over the crowd, so far she was in danger of falling off the podium. "He is for you, and He will fight for you. Now is not the time to back down. Now is not the time to surrender!"

I winced. I knew she didn't mean for her words to be political, but I could tell that the better part of the crowd—especially the teenagers—took them that way. I saw the soldiers exchanging nods and slaps on the back while the youth pumped fists. The damage had been done.

Phil abruptly came off her spiritual high. She blinked, like she'd returned to this reality and remembered who she was and where she was. She backed away from the edge of the podium and flushed bright red, but the smile remained on her face.

She turned to hand the microphone back to the pastor. He didn't take it. Instead, he put his hands out in front of him, one on top of the other, and bowed.

The room fell silent as the rest of the leadership on the platform followed suit. Slowly, like a wave rolling into the shore, the crowd copied. One by one, everyone, even the little children, stacked their hands and bent their backs, until the entire room was bowing.

Except me.

She finally caught my eye over the dipped heads of the crowd. I glared at her, knowing my opinion was clearly written on my face.

You have no idea what you've done.

"Von?"

I turned. A Chinese man about my age pushed his way towards me as the crowd began to disperse. He halted and frowned at me.

"Sorry," he said, blinking as if he'd seen a ghost. "You just look so much like your father. Nic, was it? May I call you that?"

"Please don't call me anything longer," I returned, and accepted the handshake he offered. I felt at a sore disadvantage since I couldn't return the favor of name recognition.

He mercifully helped me out. "Tang Lanzhou."

Tang—the factory owner's surname. Vague recollections of a younger Tang shadowing meetings with my father came back to me, and I realized this must be the factory owner's son. We were comparable in age, which meant we'd shared an assumed companionship while our fathers talked business and civil disobedience. To call him a "friend" would have been much too forward, but if he remembered my father, that was a step in the right direction.

"What are you doing here?" Lanzhou dropped his voice to a volume intended only for me to hear.

"Trying and failing to keep my legal dependent from starting a war" would have been the correct answer. I glanced back at the podium. The crowd had come back to life and was now swarming the platform, chattering and calling out to Phil. Everyone, especially the teenagers, was clamoring to shake her hand. Phil seemed to have forgotten that she was a walking bomb and accepted the friendship enthusiastically.

Lanzhou followed my gaze. "How do you know Blue Fire?"

I groaned. "My enemies call me 'Q,'" I admitted, and hoped that would be enough. My full involvement in Blue Fire's history—namely, that I was the nameless "governor" who had invented Red Rain—was not information I was eager to divulge.

Thankfully, Lanzhou didn't ask for more details. "And what are you two doing in Beijing?"

"Mission gone awry," I grunted, which was actually the complete truth.

He paled at the implications. "She shouldn't be here. The entire council wants her dead."

I couldn't agree more—although, I realized in a cruel irony, it wasn't an entirely accurate statement. The rest of the Beijing leadership might want Phil to hang, but Asia wanted her alive, which was even worse.

"That's actually why we're here," I said, seizing the opportunity to shift the conversation. I glanced around to make sure no one was eavesdropping before confessing, "We need to get off the grid. We're looking for Jael."

The way his eyes flickered told me I'd hit the jackpot. At least Jael *was* a real person—that was a start.

"Who told you that name?" he demanded, but not unkindly.

"Narissa."

If he knew her, he didn't let it on. "Jael's not in town right now," he said, cautiously, his eyes also taking a warning lap around the room. "But I can call one of her people."

I wasn't thrilled about the prospect of being run through this mystical woman's secretary, but it was better than anything else I had to go on at this point. "Can she help?"

"She's probably the only person who can help you." The bitter tone of his voice told me that our situation was as dire as I feared. "And for Blue Fire, she will," he added, answering my other unspoken question. Phil had been right about one thing—these people did love her.

You're all fools.

"We need to get you out of sight before she causes a scene," Lanzhou hissed.

We were well past that stage, in my opinion. I looked up and watched as a woman bowed before Phil and held out a gift; it looked like a piece of jewelry of some kind. Phil accepted the offering reverently.

"You can stay at my house. There's plenty of room." Lanzhou touched my shoulder.

I made no attempt to be polite as I shrugged out of his grasp. "We're fine, thank you. Just tell us when and where to meet Jael."

"Nic, please, I can tell you're not fine. I don't know what happened out there, but you look terrible. When was the last time you slept?"

I'd snatched a few hours last night, which might have been enough, had I not been sleeping outside, on concrete, and in the rain. I instinctively reached up to touch my unshaven chin and realized he had a point. We couldn't spend another night on the street. We needed showers and a full meal, and I needed to borrow a device so I could get online and call Ephesus.

"Fine. And thank you," I added for the sake of decorum, even though I was feeling anything but grateful.

He beamed. "It would be an honor to host you and Blue Fire."

I'm sure it would, I thought as I forced a smile.

He turned. "Come on—this way."

One night, I promised myself as I followed him through the crowd. We would stay one night so we could get online, make arrangements with Jael, and rest. Then we were leaving before Phil caused any more damage.

I looked back to see a guard hustling her off stage. *Just one night,* I repeated, *and then Blue Fire is retiring for good.*

12: PHILADELPHIA

My head swam as I received an endless stream of handshakes, bows, and salutes. It wasn't that I wasn't present in the moment; in fact, it was almost like I was *too* present. The people in front of me seemed larger than life, and all I could focus on was the expressions on their faces and the inflections in their voices—things they probably didn't even notice about themselves.

All the while, the words I'd spoken into the mic kept echoing around in my head, louder than ever, as if the Holy Spirit never stopped talking. All I could think about was how much God *loved* these people, and how precious they were to Him, and how much He wanted to protect and prosper them. I wanted to tell them all that, look each of them in the eye and remind them who their God was. But the crowd was so thick and excited that I couldn't have gotten a word in had I wanted to, so I just accepted their affection as my spirit continued to spin out of my control.

I jerked out of my stupor when a lady pressed something cold into my hands. I looked down at it: It was a beautiful bangle made of solid jade.

My heart went to my throat. "No, please," I said, pushing it back.

She smiled and closed my fingers around the jewelry. "It's a symbol of protection," she insisted. "So, when you wear it, remember that we're all praying for you."

I squeezed the bracelet over my hand and felt the weight settle on my wrist. "Thank you," I whispered, suddenly too overwhelmed to say more.

There was an eruption of chatter from the other women standing by, and I saw several pull their own bangles off their wrists. One by one, women walked up to the platform and laid their jewelry at my feet: bracelets, pendants, even earrings. My refusals fell on deaf ears. All I could do was stare at the growing pile of precious green stone and murmur endless thank you's as my emotions caved in on me like a breaking wave.

A voice came from behind me. "Blue Fire?"

I turned to see one of the pastors bowing to me. It was the one who had handed me the microphone. He was perhaps forty, with a youthful charm to his expression that wholly disagreed with his slightly grayed hair. "Tang Bowen. Do you prefer Blue Fire or Miss Smyrna?"

"Just Philadelphia, please," I said. If these people knew my secret identity, I was going to take the rare opportunity to use my birth name.

He smiled warmly. "You're to be a guest at my family's house tonight. This way, please. Don't worry, I'll send someone to collect your things."

I turned to follow him. A guard flanked me and hustled me off the stage, eliciting several cries of protest from the crowd.

Nic met us backstage, along with several more guards and another Asian businessman. One of the soldiers held out my jacket and backpack. "Your bag, miss..." He hesitated. "It's... meowing."

"Tommy!" I cried, remembering. Figuring I could get away with just about anything at this point, I unzipped my bag and took my cat into my arms. He howled in protest and tried to lunge towards Nic. I hissed a reprimand and adjusted my grip on his bony frame.

The Asian man laughed. "I see we need to set out three extra places tonight. Tang Lanzhou." Since my hands were full, he forewent a handshake and bobbed his head instead. "Our family is old friends of the Vons."

I remembered what Nic had said about the factory owner and deduced that these men must be related. The family resemblance between Bowen and Lanzhou was slight but noticeable, making me wonder if they were cousins. The knowledge that they knew Mr. Von instantly made me feel more at peace. "Very pleased to meet you," I said.

"The honor is all ours," Lanzhou returned with a smile. "Come on—you must be exhausted from your journey."

It was phrased tactfully, but I was sure our situation must be apparent. If nothing else, the pungent smell of my muddy clothing must have given it away.

The thought of a warm bath, a full meal, and a real bed made my heart dizzy. I turned to Nic as we followed the guards down the hallway. "See?" I whispered after Lanzhou and Bowen had gotten a step ahead of us. "I told you they would help us."

He didn't answer. I searched his face for a reaction, but there was none. His expression was completely blank, which either meant he'd given up—or he'd made a deliberate effort to mask his emotions.

I shook off a shiver of nervousness. We would talk later, I was sure, but even he couldn't deny that I was right. No one could deny what happened back there.

We followed the Tangs out to the docks, where I paused to hide my tattoo and put my blue contacts back in, just in case. They led us down the narrow boardwalk that flanked the river, back into the residential district. The sun was still warm in the sky, but it had dipped below the houses, silhouetting the whole street in soft pink and orange. Shutters were opened to the cooling air, and families gathered in laughing clusters on their verandas. I heard plates clattering and smelled foreign spices and was suddenly reminded how hungry I was. Tommy mewed and struggled to get down.

The Tangs led us under a quaint stone arch that opened to a small courtyard. It was a stunning traditional residence in immaculate condition. A ring of two-story wooden homes boxed in the patio. The shutters were carved with traditional geometric designs, and the balconies on the upper floors were decorated with lanterns and ornate railings. A covered veranda overlooked the canal. It held a long table, around which were gathered at least a dozen people.

"Ba!" Lanzhou called, darting ahead of us. "You won't believe who I've brought you."

The elderly man at the head of the table rose and came to meet us. Lanzhou took his hands and guided him to Nic. "This is Nic Von Nieuwenhuyse, Von's son—you remember?"

Mr. Tang's face exploded in a grin that seemed too big for his slight frame to contain. "If I didn't, that mustache would remind me. You're a spitting image—it's like he's back from the dead."

Nic hesitated, clearly waffling between familiarity and formality. He finally settled on a half bow. "Tang *Xiansheng*."

"None of that," the man snorted. He reached out and yanked Nic into a hug that looked surprisingly strong. I choked back a laugh as every muscle in Nic's body went rigid.

Mr. Tang gave him a firm pat on the back. "You have our condolences. Your father is sorely missed."

"Thank you," Nic said, and relaxed—just a little.

Mr. Tang released him. "It's wonderful to have you back. What brings you to Beijing?"

Nic put up his hand. "We're not staying long—"

Bowen spoke on top of him. "That's our other surprise." He gently shoved me forward. "Blue Fire has come to honor our house tonight."

The other family members clustered around with a whisper of surprise. "Hi," I managed, having no idea what etiquette would be appropriate. "Honored to meet you."

The senior Tang beamed. "The honor is all ours," he said, and bowed. His family copied him.

"Please, that's not necessary," I begged. I was a little miffed that Nic, the one person who *didn't* want a hug, was the only one who got one. I squeezed Tommy for consolation—a little too hard for his tastes. He yelped and dug all of his claws into my arm. I instinctively let go, and he leapt to the ground and darted across the courtyard.

"Tommy!" I cried. Logically, I knew he was just a stray, but it still hurt to be rejected so quickly.

"Don't worry, he'll come home when he's ready," Lanzhou assured me with a chuckle.

"Which is hopefully never," Nic muttered. I glared at him, but he intentionally looked elsewhere.

An elegant older woman—Mrs. Tang, I assumed—stepped forward. "Come," she said to me while beckoning at two other female family members. "Let's get you cleaned up."

They led me upstairs to a bathroom, where I took an absolutely heavenly shower. Despite the fact that the bathroom was ancient—the water was slightly cold and tasted metallic—I'd never been so grateful for running water in my life. While I scrubbed and conditioned my hair, Mrs. Tang threw my disgraced outfit in the wash and sent a niece to scrounge up a change of clothes for me. The shorts and t-shirt she brought barely fit, but I was thrilled to be wearing something that smelled of soap instead of sweat. I slid on the borrowed pair of house shoes and went to join the family on the veranda.

Night was falling, and a cool breeze swept across the open deck. The canal glowed orange-red with the light from a hundred lanterns. The windows on almost every house along the block were open, allowing the laughter and chatter of the neighbors to mingle with ours.

We all crammed around the long wooden table while Mrs. Tang served a vibrant feast that never seemed to end. There were heaps of steamed rice, mounds of colorful sauteed vegetables, and crispy chunks of tofu simmering in red-hot sauce. There were more dumplings than I could count and a fish that had been broiled whole. I sat between two of the Tang daughters, who giggled and showed me how to use chopsticks while we all ate from the same bowls in communal harmony.

Nic, for his part, looked significantly less grumpy with his hair washed and his mustache and goatee returned to their natural order. He wasn't very talkative; he only engaged when Lanzhou cornered him with a question. But he ate enthusiastically and seemed less annoyed with the world (and me) than usual.

Conversation at the table steered mercifully clear of politics, in part because we were outside within potential earshot of the neighbors. But as soon as the younger family members had wandered off, Bowen lured me into the kitchen under the pretense of washing dishes.

"Is everything all right?" he said in a tone barely loud enough to be heard over the water running in the sink.

I switched the faucet off and plunged my hands into the soapy water. "You're going to need to be more specific."

"With Operation Blue Fire." He dropped another plate into the sink, causing a tuft of bubbles to float away. "I saw your last video, and it's been over a week since you were online. Is there something we should know?"

I wished I had an answer for him, but the truth—that my allies had tried to kill me and we were on the run from the most powerful woman in China—seemed like information I shouldn't reveal yet. "Everything's under control," I said, which was probably the biggest lie I'd ever told.

"What in the world are you doing? Get out of the kitchen! You're our guest!" Lanzhou appeared in the doorway with a stack of bowls.

"I don't mind," I protested. In fact, doing mundane chores sounded relaxing.

He wasn't having it and elbowed me out of the way. "Let me handle this. I can do the dishes—we need you to focus on other things."

Bowen handed me a towel. "He's right. You need to record a video. People are talking."

I looked down at my hands and took my time wiping away every last trace of soap. "What are they saying?"

"That you quit." Bowen's statement was factual, without any accusation, but I could hear the uncertainty in his voice. "They're saying you got scared and the operation is canceled."

My heart shattered as he confirmed my worst fears. The movement was failing—and it was all because of me. All because I listened to Jayde instead of the Holy Spirit.

But it wasn't too late, was it? "The operation's still on," I insisted, and desperately hoped it was true.

"Then tell them that. Please," Bowen pleaded. "They need to hear from you. I… need to hear from you."

I looked up to find him staring at me. Abruptly, he chuckled.

"What?" I prodded.

He grinned boyishly. "Sorry, I just still can't believe *Blue Fire* is in my kitchen."

"And you almost made her wash the dishes," Lanzhou chided.

"I volunteered," I reminded him, and we all shared a laugh.

Bowen sobered and leaned against the cold oven. "Why are you really in Beijing? I know Nic didn't come just to see us."

That's an understatement. I swallowed and struggled to come up with a plausible excuse.

"Nic said it was a mission gone awry," Lanzhou volunteered when I went silent for too long.

That was certainly one way to put it. "I can't tell you," I managed, which was, regrettably, the truth.

"We understand," Lanzhou said. His voice was slow and gentle, as if I was a scared rabbit that might bolt. "We just want to help if we can."

"You can trust us—you can trust all of us," Bowen added, too quickly. "My entire congregation supports the operation. I've got six more churches across the city willing to move, and several more in nearby provinces. All you have to do is say the word."

My heart started beating fast but steady, like my pulse had slipped into a higher gear. The thought that there were churches in Beijing—whole congregations of people I'd never met—that supported me made my head spin. Jayde had told me that the operation had global support, but it was just a statistic, the faceless analytics on my videos. Now I had seen it with my own eyes.

I twirled the jade bangle around my wrist. These people were willing to risk their lives for a cause *I* started. Was I really going to drop off the grid and leave them all behind? Did God really give me all of this influence and power just to have me throw it away? Was Blue Fire really a mistake?

Bowen didn't seem to think so. "Please, if there's ever anything you need, just say so."

What I needed was to talk to somebody. Someone who understood me and believed I was destined to do good in the world. Someone who believed that God had been working miraculously in my life.

And that person was not Nic.

"I need to get online," I said, looking up. "And I can't make a mark on my file. Do you have a device I can borrow?"

"Of course. Follow me." Bowen turned and led the way out of the kitchen.

The night had grown dark, and the rest of the family had retired to bed—as had Nic, apparently. Both the veranda and the courtyard were empty as I followed Bowen to the hall that faced the street. He fetched a tablet from a locked drawer in Mr. Tang's study, then led me up the stairs to the second floor. The narrow corridor was divided into several small bedrooms, but the cramped space was no less elegant than the rest of the house. The dark wood paneling, silkscreen doors, and carved shutters gave the dimly lit hallway the air of a temple.

"I put your belongings in here." Bowen opened the door closest to the stairs. "I believe Nic's staying at the end of the hall."

I glanced down the hallway. There was no light shining from under the door; had he fallen asleep already?

"Thank you," I said, turning back to Bowen. "For everything."

He beamed. "Anything for Blue Fire. Most of the family sleeps in the hall on the other side of the courtyard—come get us if you need anything."

I smiled gratefully. He gave a slight bow and descended the stairs.

I stepped into the bedroom and shut the door behind me. The room was narrow but beautifully decorated. The modest shelf bed was carved with silhouettes of dragons and clouds, and the nightstand and wardrobe were solid dark mahogany. The linens were muted shades of blue and turquoise, making the pile of pillows look like a pool of water. The silkscreen door to the tiny private balcony was open, filling the room with cool night air and the steady sound of the river.

I took a deep breath and let the peace of the quiet room wash over me. I felt my jaw unclench while the muscles all along my spine relaxed. It was as if my body, for the first time in three days, abruptly realized that we could stop running. We would be safe here—at least for tonight. *Thank you, Jesus.*

I sank down on the edge of the bed. Instantly, the cocoon of silk and cotton threatened to pull me in. I would have fallen asleep right then if my mind weren't fixated on more pressing matters.

I turned on the tablet, installed the messaging app Nic always used, and created a dummy profile. Thankfully, I had Stanyard's username memorized. I had no idea who this tablet was registered to or how good the Tangs' internet protection was, so I sent a generic message and hoped he wouldn't ignore the unfamiliar username.

IT'S ME. IS IT SAFE TO TALK?

I gripped the device, praying. Almost immediately, his avatar flashed green, and the device trilled.

I answered. "Stanyard!" I gasped, almost before my audio and video had connected.

"Philadelphia! Oh, praise God." His video came on, bringing me face to face with my best friend. He shoved his headphones back, causing his wild brown hair to spring up in all directions. It was so cute that I almost cried. "You're okay," he said, the inflection somewhere between a statement and a question.

"Yes, I promise. We're in a safe place, and Nic's with me." I searched his image, wishing he wasn't so far away. Stanyard would give me the hug I so desperately needed—and a kiss, if I were so inclined. "Are you okay? Where are you?"

"I'm fine," he insisted. "I'm on base right now."

I gasped. Base was the last place he should be. "Stanyard! You need to get out of there! Jayde—"

Someone else spoke in the background. "Is that her?"

I stiffened; I knew that Russian accent all too well. "Get away from him!"

He did the exact opposite. Lev shoved his way into the frame, leaning over Stanyard's shoulder and practically pushing my boyfriend out of the shot.

My blood ran hot and cold as I vacillated between betrayal and anger. Lev was Jayde's lackey, the very person who was supposed to pull the trigger if I failed the mission. Of all the people on base, he was the one I trusted the least; I knew where his loyalties lay. "Don't touch him!" I hissed.

Lev tipped his head to the side and squinted his faded blue eyes in that lost, pitiful expression that used to make me feel sorry for him. "But I wasn't—"

"No," I snapped. "You know what you did. How could you?"

"Whoa, Phil, it's okay." Stanyard put himself back in the center of the camera and tried to regain control of the situation. "He's with me. He told me everything."

"What?"

"As soon as you guys left, he told me what was going on. He would never have hurt me, Phil."

"But…" That revelation should have made me feel relieved—and it did—but it also made me more confused. "Why didn't he stop Jayde? He could have prevented all of this."

Lev answered for himself. "I didn't know what Jayde would do to you."

I swallowed. Stanyard handed him the device so I could see Lev's face as he continued. "He's a violent man, and I didn't know what he would do if I defied him. So I waited until you were gone."

"He sent false reports to Jayde so he would think everything was under control," Stanyard added. "It bought us time so Nic could get to you."

I took a deep breath as one of the fractured pieces of my life was made whole again: Lev *did* care, and he was every bit the innocent youth I thought he was. "Thank you," I said with as much sincerity and respect as I could.

His face twitched in a small smile. "I'm loyal to you, thunderbird," he said, and saluted.

Stanyard took the device back. I waited until Lev had walked away before speaking. "Does everybody know?"

Stanyard nodded. "The entire base knows what happened. Tower didn't tell them all the details, but he made it clear that Jayde forced you into a rogue mission against your will. Everyone's on your side."

I leaned my head against the bedpost as this new reality coalesced. Operation Blue Fire truly *was* still on schedule. Nothing had changed, not really. Jayde was dangerous, yes, but he was one man with limited supporters. If I released a statement before he did, I could remove him from power and pick the movement up where it left off.

"I need to record a video," I declared, sitting up.

"I agree," Stanyard said, but his voice had that slow pitch to it that told me he had reservations. "But what are you going to say?"

"That the operation is still on schedule. That Blue Fire is back. Don't you see? We can still do this." I searched his face, desperately hoping I wouldn't see doubt and disappointment. I got enough of that from Nic.

There wasn't any, but he still looked nervous as he replied, "I do see. But Phil—you're in Beijing. It's *not* safe there."

Maybe it wasn't—but that didn't mean I was without help. "I know, but Stanyard, there's *thousands* of people who support me here. I met a pastor today; he says he's got a dozen churches ready to move. And he's just the first person I talked to."

Stanyard's compassionate brown eyes went wide with the reverence that statement deserved. "What are you suggesting?"

I chewed my lip as the excitement swirled around in my head with nowhere to land. "I don't know. I just know this can't all be a mistake."

"I don't think it is," he agreed.

I struggled to detangle my thoughts from the guilt and shame that tainted them. "I know Nic thinks I should never have gone back to Earth, but... I just can't believe that God set this all up for nothing. I know trying to kill the General was a mistake, but... what if the rest wasn't?"

It had been Jayde's idea to assassinate the General, but all the events leading up to that had been out of his control. Andromeda Nolan, Asia, the invite to the party. Even now, I questioned whether Asia was truly interested in Nic's affections. Surely, there was more to her role in this; what if God had been pulling the strings the entire time?

Stanyard was silent for a long moment as we both let those thoughts run their course. "What are you saying?" he prodded.

It wasn't an accusation; it was an invitation. He knew what I was thinking, but I had to say it for myself.

"I'm saying... maybe I am supposed to be in Beijing."

I pinched my eyes shut as that admission caused the events of the past few weeks to warp and refocus, this time with entirely different colors.

"I don't know," Stanyard admitted with gentle honesty. "But whatever you do, I'll support you."

I opened my eyes and looked down at the screen. "Thank you." *This is why I love you.*

"Just promise me one thing. Before you do anything, talk to Nic."

I cringed, and he saw. "I know he's a pain sometimes, but he knows more about Beijing politics than the rest of us put together. He knows what you're dealing with, and he knows the city."

"I know, and I want to talk to him," I said, and it was the truth. "It's just... I feel like he hates everything about the revolution. And he certainly doesn't believe God's involved."

My heart ached at my own words. If only Nic would give God another chance, then, surely, he'd see what I saw.

"I know," Stanyard echoed. "But he cares about you."

I sighed. I couldn't deny that.

"I'm not saying take his word as the gospel, but... he wouldn't have come all the way back to Earth to save you if he didn't care. He sees something in you—even if it's not what you see."

I let the silence hang as I considered that.

"Plus... I'd feel a lot better if you talked to him."

I looked back down at the screen. Stanyard was smiling, but I could see the pain etched in the creases around his lips. "I'm sorry, Stanyard," I whispered. "For lying and leaving you out of the conversation."

"I know you are."

"Are you... mad?" I braced myself for his answer.

"It's fine," he said, but the look in his eyes told me he was holding back just because he didn't want to hurt me.

"No, tell me, please." I didn't really want to hear it, but I had to know. I couldn't live with open wounds between Stanyard and me. Not like I did with my father.

"I'd be lying if I said it didn't hurt when I found out you changed your mind literally *ten minutes* after we'd talked about it." Some of the pain slipped into his voice, and he took a breath, long and deep. "But that's between me and the Lord. It's not your job to manage my feelings."

I struggled to accept that as I marveled, yet again, at the work Jesus had done in Stanyard's life. This was not the same bitter teen I'd known in high school.

"Do you forgive me?" I asked after a moment.

"Yes," he said without hesitation, bringing our relationship full circle as we traded places. "Of course, I do."

I sank back against the pillows and let the strength of our relationship break my fall—again. "I love you so much. And I miss you."

"You have *no* idea how much I miss you." His eyes danced as he allowed a broad grin to take over his face. "When you get back, you owe me a first date. Like a real one."

I sucked in my breath as the butterflies did their elated dance in my stomach. A date? I tried to imagine what it would be like to eat at a candlelit table, or go to the movies, or walk in the park—but the images seemed fuzzy, like a watercolor illustration. Our relationship had been so plagued by fear and terror and pain—not to mention that one time I almost shot him in the face—that I couldn't even imagine what it would be like to just *date*. To just enjoy life.

"Deal," I said, and found myself blushing. The smile he was giving me wasn't making it easy for me to keep my composure.

Abruptly, I remembered who else was back in Boston. I sat up. "How's Dad?"

Stanyard hesitated, and I panicked. "What's wrong?"

"Nothing," he said, putting a hand up. "That's just it. He's doing *great*. Mrs. Nolan woke him up a few days ago, and he's making excellent progress."

"Really?" I gasped. All the air was choked out of my lungs as a hundred forgotten hopes suddenly resurrected in my soul. Was it possible that my dad might get to live a normal life? Had God given me my father back?

"He doesn't remember any people," Stanyard quickly clarified, "but he's gotten a lot of his vocabulary back, and he's flying through physical therapy. Andes installed some kind of brain implant, and he's been working with... what's his name? Data? I think he's the one who programmed your chip."

I flinched but nodded. Data was one of the many members of the Boston underground—a prominent one, judging by how active he had been on the radio. He was also a powerful programmer and was the one who had procured the General Secretary's DNA and coded the kill chip in my palm.

Stanyard didn't seem bothered by the man's resume. "They've both been working with him, and whatever they're doing is really helping. He was a different person this morning."

That was great news to me, but I caught the hitch in Stanyard's voice. "What is it?"

His eyes took a lap around the room, like they always did when he was hesitant to admit something. "I don't know. It's kind of scary how fast he's improving. Mrs. Nolan doesn't like it."

"Well, she doesn't believe in miracles." I did. *Thank you, Jesus.* "Can I see him?"

Stanyard grimaced. "I don't think that's a good idea tonight. He won't remember you, and he's still very disoriented. He was kind of... surly when I talked to him earlier."

My soul ached, but I didn't blame my father for his attitude. After all, he had just been raised from the dead and had no idea who he was, let alone who any of the people around him were. That would be terrifying, lonely, and frustrating.

I knew it was going to take time to put my father back together, even with all this progress. Would he ever regain his memories? I dared, for the first time in weeks, to hope that might be possible. But even if he didn't, at least he would have a chance at a dignified life. And that was all I could ask for.

"Tell him I love him," I said, blinking away tears that weren't quite happy. "Even if he doesn't know who I am."

Stanyard nodded.

I heard footsteps creaking in the hall and stood up. "I think Nic's awake—I'm going to go talk to him."

Stanyard nodded approvingly. "When can you call me again?"

"I don't know how long we're staying here, but it's definitely for tonight. I can call you when I get up."

"I'd like that a lot. I love you, Philadelphia."

I savored the sweet tone of his voice before returning the affection. "I love you too."

13: NIC

For a few surreal hours, it was as though the last twenty years had never happened.

Without waiting for permission, the Tangs assimilated me back into the fold. Lanzhou peppered me with questions as if we were under a moral obligation to catch up, while Mr. Tang treated me exactly as he would my father. They inquired about my work on Mars, and Mrs. Tang was mortified to learn that I was still romantically unattached. There was teasing and reminiscing and altogether too much laughter. The whole family acted as if nothing had changed.

As if I hadn't changed.

I excused myself as soon as I could without arousing suspicion. I pulled Lanzhou aside, out of earshot of his younger relatives. "I need to borrow a device."

He nodded and led me across the courtyard to his father's study. "Is your file marked?" he guessed, not easily fooled.

"Let's just say some people aren't happy about my involvement with Blue Fire."

He grunted and stooped to unlock the secret drawer hidden at the bottom of his father's massive desk. "I talked to Jael. She said it might be a few days before she can get here herself, but she's sending her people tomorrow."

A few days? There was no way I was staying in one place for that long. A thousand starry-eyed churchgoers knew Philadelphia was in the area; it was only a matter of time before word got out and Asia made her move. I wasn't going to leave the lights on for her.

My objections must have made it onto my face, because Lanzhou looked up and spoke emphatically. "I promise you're safe here."

"I might be," I said by way of concession, "but keeping Phil quiet is like trying to hide a cackle of starved hyenas. Trust me, I've tried."

He was not deterred by my visceral metaphor. "My father has bought off half the local police force to keep the church safe. He can cover Blue Fire for a couple of nights." He pulled out a tablet and locked the drawer. "I asked a few of the guards from the factory to come watch the house tonight if that makes you feel better."

It did, actually. But I wasn't about to admit it, so I changed the subject. "How protected is your internet traffic?"

"Well enough." He turned the tablet on and held it out to me. "Jael has 'tweaked' our router as a thank-you for what we're doing for the church, so most of our traffic bypasses the algorithm. Don't go logging into any government sites, but as long as you use this device, your calls won't be recorded."

That was all I needed to hear. I took the device, nodded a goodnight, and went to my room on the second floor. It was at the end of the hall, as far away from other people as possible—just where I liked it.

Phil hadn't made it up to her room at the top of the stairs yet. She was probably still in the kitchen, soaking up the companionship like a well-adjusted human. She and I needed to have a talk, but not before I called Ephesus.

I shut and latched my bedroom door and turned off the lights, hoping that would deter any intrusion. I had a suspicion that Asia knew about all my accounts, even the encrypted ones, so I installed a messaging app and created a dummy profile. I sent Ephesus a message and sat back to wait. If my calculations were correct, it should be about the same time at the base on Mars as it was in Beijing, which meant he was hopefully awake and paying attention to his phone.

It took him long enough—about fifteen minutes—but he eventually called me back. "Taking the night off?" I chided, not being shy with my annoyance.

"No, but I have a base to run." There was a beat before he enabled video, as if he wasn't sure if he wanted to see my face.

"Is everything all right? Have you had any trouble? Have you checked on the ionators in Wing 56 recently? They've been buggy—and don't forget the gravity augmenter in Wing 43 needs to be manually calibrated every six weeks."

Ephesus blinked. "Miss me, huh?"

"You? No. The base, yes." This was more emotional transparency than I was comfortable sharing with Ephesus, but I would have given anything to be sitting at my desk on Mars and slogging through mundane emails right now. I would have even volunteered to do paperwork.

"The base is fine," Ephesus insisted as he settled down in a desk chair. "As is Cea, in case you were going to ask."

"I wasn't. I'm quite confident that you're taking *excellent* care of her."

He smiled, as if he took that as a compliment. In a way, it was.

"Where's Phil?" he demanded after he'd stopped daydreaming about his new wife.

As if in answer, I heard a door shut further down the hall, and muffled voices came through the thin paneling. "Sounds like she's in the other room making kissy faces at her boyfriend."

"Stanyard?"

I rolled my eyes. As if Phil would give the time of day to literally anyone else.

"Well, tell her to call me."

I murmured to myself as the facts of the situation made themselves apparent. "Fascinating."

"I think what you meant to say was, 'Of course, brother-in-law.'"

"First of all, I don't care what the paper says; I'm not calling you that. Second of all, I just made the unfortunate deduction that she must *really* be in love with him."

"Well yeah," Ephesus fussed. "They've known each other since like the first grade. I'm not surprised—"

"Not that," I cut him off with a groan. Ephesus's innocence would be adorable—if he weren't a full-grown man. "I mean, she's only been online twice in the last seventy-two hours, and both times, she's chosen to call him instead of you."

We both let that fact marinate in the silence. Ephesus, because he was stunned by my flawless tact. Me, because I finally realized that this relationship *was* serious. And if I didn't want Phil to run off and elope without involving me—like her brother did—I'd better start taking it seriously.

Ephesus recovered from the slight. "Do me a favor and stay on Earth."

I sighed and brought my focus back to more immediate problems. "I may not have a choice."

Using as few gory details as possible, I briefed Ephesus on the issues regarding my file and my involvement with Asia.

He, naturally, took the opportunity to antagonize me. "Wow, didn't realize you were such a heartthrob."

"It's the facial hair. You should try it sometime," I returned, even though I was aware of the irony. My mustache was the one part about me that Asia *didn't* like. "But, even though I'm sure she's already started picking out curtains, I don't think it's me she wants. I think it's your sister."

Ephesus knotted his eyebrows together and waited for me to elaborate.

"I think she's using me as leverage to make sure Phil doesn't leave the city. The Nolans, the party invite—I think this was all an elaborate set-up to get Phil to Beijing."

"I have to admit that makes a lot more sense than her wanting revenge for unrequited love," Ephesus consented. "But what could she possibly want Phil for?"

"That's what I haven't figured out yet."

"I'm shocked," Ephesus said in a tone that suggested he actually was.

"I've been a little preoccupied with not dying."

"Then let's put our brains together. What do you know about Asia?"

"A lot of things I'd rather forget," I admitted. "But first and foremost, she's not stupid. She knows about Phil's multiple personalities, and she knows Jayde is with the underground. I'm sure she realized Phil had ulterior motives for coming to Beijing."

"She was going to let it happen," Ephesus surmised. "But why? What does she have to gain?"

Everything.

As soon as he said it, I knew.

"She wanted Phil to pull the trigger," I explained, spelling it out for both of us. "She wanted her father to die. She wants war."

Asia wanted power—she always had. But if she had tried to depose the General directly, she would have ignited resistance from the council and her father's loyalists. She would have risked weakening the entire government, never mind the heyday the press would have had with her reputation. But if she could get Phil to start a war—or, better yet, assassinate the General—then she could seize power while barely lifting a finger. All the while, she could unite the government and the press against those pesky "unassimilated."

After all, if there was one thing Asia hated, it was an unnecessary mess.

Ephesus broke the heavy silence. "We need to get Phil off that planet."

"I couldn't agree more, but that's going to be easier said than done when Asia isn't the only one who wants her to start a war."

His eyes darkened. "Do you think the underground will try to keep her there?"

I glanced out the window at the shadowy courtyard, reassuring myself that no one was within earshot. "I don't know, but they certainly won't be happy when they find out she's retiring for good."

And neither will the Lord, I abruptly remembered with a punch to the gut.

"What can I do to help?" Ephesus unwittingly interrupted.

"Sadly, probably nothing." I tried to turn my thoughts back to the conversation at hand, but it was like slogging through wet concrete. "There's a woman here who can supposedly get us new files without Asia knowing. I'm not optimistic, but I'm going to at least give her until tomorrow."

"And if she fails to deliver?"

"Then I need you working on backup plans. Money isn't the problem—Phil could buy the entire planet of Mars if she wanted." I snorted at the irony of that. "The problem is figuring out a way to transfer the money so that there is absolutely no electronic trail linking our old files to our new ones. Asia's watching our accounts like a hawk—if we transfer even a penny, she's going to investigate."

"So you need a creative programmer," Ephesus suggested.

"No, I need a *genius* programmer." I arched my eyebrow and waited for him to take the invitation.

He beamed. "I'm flattered."

"Don't let it go to your head. We also need a technician who's good about covering his tracks. We can't use Andes; Asia knows we've worked with him before."

"I'm on it," Ephesus declared. I saw him start typing in the background.

"Thank you," I said, and meant it. I paused and leaned my ear towards the wall; I could still hear Phil chattering away. I'd better go in there and get my obligatory lecture out of the way before she fell asleep. "I need to go," I announced to Ephesus.

"Call me tomorrow with an update," he said, sounding uncannily like me.

I figured our relationship had progressed to the point where we didn't need to bother with paltry etiquette like goodbyes, so I hung up.

Setting the tablet aside, I opened my door and started down the hall. Phil must have been hit with the same brain wave, because at that moment she came out of her room.

"Nic." She darted over and met me halfway. "Can we talk?"

"We're about to."

She looked down and fidgeted, apparently losing her nerve. "It's about today."

How nice of her to volunteer the subject. "Yes, about that." I crossed my arms, bracing myself for her pitiful excuses. "You deliberately disobeyed me."

She riffled through her repertoire of arguments and settled on the weakest one. "But I didn't... I didn't mean to."

"I'm going to need you to backspace that sentence and try again, because there was nothing unintentional about what you did. I explicitly told you not to identify yourself as Blue Fire. Do you have any idea how dangerous that was?" I fought to keep the pain out of my voice. Why couldn't she just listen to me for once? Did she really not see how much danger she was putting both of us in?

"I know, I know, I just... didn't want him to pull up your file and cause a scene."

"So you went and caused a bigger scene? Phil, you just identified yourself in front of a thousand people, and we don't know a single one of them. How do you know one of them isn't going to tell the police? And don't say it's because they all go to church."

The way she snapped her mouth shut told me that's exactly what she had been planning to say.

I rubbed my temples; I could already feel the pressure headache coming on, and we'd only been talking for sixty seconds. "Phil, you can't trust someone just because they go to church—or because they claim to be part of the underground."

"Maybe." She swallowed and made her voice calm and strong, as if that would impress me. "But that doesn't mean we're not in this together."

"No, that's *exactly* what that means."

"No, Nic, you don't understand! This is real—the revolution is real. They really believe in me."

"It's their funeral."

She clenched her fists, and her ears flushed red. "Nic, this isn't a joke! They trust me, and they *will* follow me. All I have to do is say the word."

"Which is exactly why you should keep your mouth shut." I stopped when I realized this conversation was starting to sound exactly like the arguments we'd had a dozen times before. And as a scientist, I knew firsthand that the quickest way to prove yourself an idiot was to do the same actions and expect a different result.

I took a deep breath and decided to try something revolutionary: softening my voice. "Phil, I'm not denying that the movement exists. I'm saying you need to put a stop to it before it gets out of hand."

She started to speak, but I put up a hand to stop her. "I know you think this is the solution, but it's not. You won't save a single Christian by starting a rebellion. The only person who will benefit from war is Asia."

She went silent, staring at the floor as if she were, for once, considering my words. I tried to close and lock the door while I had the opportunity. "She's using you, Phil. You are not in control. She is."

"No. She's not," Phil said, barely a whisper. She looked up. "God is."

I gaped at her. I couldn't decide which was more astounding: the fact that she was ignoring everything I said, or the fact that she'd just pulled the God-card on me.

She prattled on before I could recover. "I know you don't see the world the way I do, but there's no way this can't be God. There's just too much that has happened for this to be a crazy accident. Maybe that's not how you see it, but that's what I believe."

What a basal thing to accuse me of. The problem wasn't that I didn't see. The problem was that I saw too much.

"I think… I believe that God wanted this to happen. I believe He wants me to be Blue Fire." She straightened, her voice full of sickening confidence. "Everything that's happened these last six months has lined up to bring me here—my dad, Wing 74, Thames, even the invite to that stupid party."

I wanted to refute her, to knock the legs out from under her bravado before she did something foolish. But I couldn't come up with the words fast enough. Not when I knew she was right.

"I know trying to kill the General was a mistake, but… what if the rest wasn't? What if I am supposed to be Blue Fire? What if I am supposed to be on Earth? What if this operation is the right thing to do? What if… what if I was supposed to come to Beijing?"

She hesitated, and I could see the gears turning, her face twitching as she followed the thoughts to their logical conclusion. I knew that if I didn't shut her down right now, she'd see what I saw: that she was supposed to go to Nineveh.

And I would rather spend a hundred years in the belly of a whale than risk my life—or hers—trying to save this cursed city.

Unfortunately, I knew Phil lacked a healthy fear of death, so scaring her into quitting wouldn't work. If I wanted her to give up, I had to convince her that this *wasn't* the right thing to do.

For better or for worse, I knew exactly how to accomplish that.

"No, Phil," I said, drawing myself to my full height. "You weren't."

She started to retaliate, but I cut her off. "I know you think this is God, but do you know what I see?" I spoke slowly and deliberately, laying each word out in the open so that there would be no room for debate. "I see a foolish, impulsive teenage girl who's being used by the government to start a war. All those 'miracles' you talk about? They're just proof that Asia has been controlling the game for a very long time. She brought your family to Mars. She convinced the Nolans to adopt you. She invited you to the party. She let you play out your thunderbird fantasy—and you know why? Because she wanted you to do it."

Phil slowly shut her mouth and clenched her jaw.

I dug the grave deeper. "She wanted you to kill her father because she wanted to take his place. Your little insurrection would have given her the perfect excuse to seize power without even having to get up from her desk. She would have become the next dictator and rewritten the laws the way she wants them— and I guarantee you there isn't room for Christians in her perfect world."

I laughed joylessly when I realized how true that was. "Asia would have killed them all. She would have ended the reassimilation program for good—and your violent rebellion would have given her the perfect excuse. She would have slaughtered them. Do you really think that's what God wanted you to do?"

I saw the tears well up in Phil's eyes and knew I had won. Not wanting to take chances, I braced myself and drove the last nail in the coffin.

"I said it once, and I'll say it a dozen times until you finally get it through your head: You are not a hero. God did not choose you for anything. He had nothing to do with you becoming 'Blue Fire.' You made that up. You let your moment of fame go to your head, and you almost got us all killed. You're a fool, Philadelphia, and you'd be dead if I hadn't come to rescue you."

A sob escaped her lips. She slapped her hands over her mouth and stared down at the ground as her whole body started to shake.

I looked away. The deed was done.

"Go to your room," I ordered.

She obeyed me, a little too literally. She turned and ran down the hall, slamming the door so hard the whole house seemed to groan.

Something meowed. I looked down to see that stupid cat tangling himself around my legs.

Of course, of all the things I *didn't* want to follow me home.

I kicked him away. "Go comfort her," I snapped. Then I turned and locked myself in my room.

I closed my eyes and leaned against the door, but no sooner had the silence returned than it was broken by the sound of pitiful sobbing from outside.

I unwillingly walked to the window. Phil was on her balcony, crying. She huddled against the railing with her face on her knees, doing a terrible job of muffling her sobs.

I slammed and latched my shutters, dampening the sound. Fishing my laptop and a pair of earbuds out of my backpack, I returned to the bed. I plugged in and queued up an album I'd stealthily downloaded while at Narissa's shop. The comforting sound of Bruno Mars instantly drowned out the world.

I leaned back on the pillow and closed my eyes. Phil would get over herself. She just needed a few hours to cry it off, like she always did, and then she'd see the truth of what I was saying. We'd meet with Jael's people tomorrow, and if they couldn't help us, I'd steal a device from the Tangs and head to the country. I'd have to be careful, but as long as I didn't let my distrust slip at breakfast, I was confident I could fool them long enough to get Phil out of town.

And then we could finally leave Earth—and the revolution— behind for good.

14: PHILADELPHIA

I didn't want to cry, but I didn't know what else to do. There was nothing I could say, nothing I could do, that would make anything right in the world.

So I huddled on the balcony, my back to the cold wooden wall, and sobbed while my universe collapsed. All the camaraderie I thought I'd developed with Nic over the past few days went up in smoke like matchsticks, lit on fire with a few choice words.

I knew what he thought of me. No matter how many times I apologized, no matter how many times I tried to make it right, I would always be the stupid, petulant teenager who ruined his life. I was foolish, arrogant, and good for nothing. I was dead weight, a burden he'd decided to shoulder because he felt sorry for me.

And nothing I could ever do or say would ever change that.

I finally understood what Stanyard meant when he said he was "giving me his weapons." He needed to know that I was truly forgiving him and wouldn't throw his past betrayal in his face every time he slipped up.

Now Nic was doing the same thing. He had all my weapons, and he wasn't afraid to use them. He hadn't forgiven me.

And, if today was any indication, he never would.

But even worse than the rejection was the cold, slippery feeling that was seeping into the corners of my mind. It was like a shadow, bleeding into my subconscious and breaking my reality apart at the edges like a cliff crumbling into the sea.

What if... what if Nic is right? What if this isn't God?

Something creaked behind me. I jumped and whipped around, but there was nothing there. The bedroom was dark and empty, the open door to the hallway drifting in the breeze.

Wait. My blood froze as I processed what I was seeing. I'd closed the door when I'd come in.

Before I could register what that meant, a large hand closed around my arm.

I started to scream, but another hand slapped over my mouth and stifled the sound. Someone big and bulky with clomping footsteps hauled me up and dragged me back into the room. Several large figures—men—crowded around me, but I couldn't make out any faces in the darkness. I shouted and squirmed against the man who held me, but it didn't do any good.

One of them wrestled my arm out of my jacket sleeve. I flinched as something sharp stabbed my upper arm. I twisted my head just in time to see one of the men yank a syringe out of my shoulder.

Blood pounded in my ears and made the room flash wild colors. *Oh God, oh God, help me!*

Someone started counting down ominously under his breath. At first, nothing happened, so I used my last window of sanity to slam my heel into my captor's shin. His hold loosened as he grunted. I managed to wrench away—just as the first wave of dizziness hit.

I tripped over the stool at the foot of the bed and crashed to the floor. I struggled to brace my hands on the wood and push myself up, but the room was spinning, spinning. I vomited without warning. I managed to roll away, but the world continued to tumble even after I stopped moving, like a can rolling downhill.

"Nic," I managed, but my voice came out weak, slurred.

"Nic can't help you now, princess," one of them grunted. There were footsteps pounding in all directions, and whispered orders, and cold hands sliding under me and picking me up. I tried to fight, but none of my nerves responded. All I could feel was a dense darkness overtaking me, like an ocean wave sweeping me under.

The last thing I registered before the world went black was a male voice I thought I recognized. "Welcome back, Blue Fire."

15: NIC

I woke to the sound of that stupid cat scratching at my bedroom door.

I knew that's what it was before I even came to full consciousness. The irritating sound of his outstretched nails grinding on the wood ripped into my sleep and shredded it like a napkin. It wasn't a light scratching, either; it sounded like he was peeling off chunks of the door with his claws.

I rolled over and put my arm over my ear. I never should have let Phil keep the dumb thing. Hopefully our hosts wouldn't charge us damages.

There was a brief respite, as if the cat had heard the bed creak and was waiting for me to get up. When the door did not open, he resumed his demands. This time, he added incessant meowing. Actually, *howling* would be a more accurate description of the blood-curdling sound the animal was producing.

I threw the blanket aside and stood up with a curse. I slammed the door open. "Get lost," I shouted, using colorful language I hoped he would appreciate.

He blinked up at me, tail flicking like a question mark. Then, as if satisfied I was fully awake, he took off.

I leaned out and watched him tear down the hallway. He nearly collided into Phil's door, which stood open.

I sighed. If Phil was up, I may as well be up. Time to face each other, get her morning dose of teenage angst out of the way, and then talk to Lanzhou about setting up a meeting with Jael. The sooner we could get new files, the sooner we could get out of here.

I returned to my bedroom and took sixty seconds to cull my mustache, straighten my hair, and put on a pair of house shoes. Then I strapped my holster under my arm and concealed it beneath my jacket. I knew I wouldn't need my gun at breakfast, but I wasn't about to leave the weapon unattended.

The house was oddly silent as I walked down to Phil's room. The only sound in the hallway was my footsteps creaking on the ancient boards.

I stood behind the open door and rapped it with my knuckles. No answer.

"Phil?" I ventured.

Still nothing. I pushed the door aside and saw that the room was empty. In fact, it looked like it hadn't been slept in at all. The bedsheets were still neatly tucked into the mattress, and the pillows were all fluffed. Had she cried herself to sleep on the balcony? I wouldn't put it past her.

I took a step into the room. The door to the balcony was open, but she wasn't outside. A quick scan revealed that her little black backpack was sitting on the nightstand.

I picked it up and unzipped it. Everything was in there, including the phone.

Something rolled on the floor behind me. I turned to see that stupid cat playing with something in the corner. He batted it back and forth as he sprang about, tail hairs on end.

I walked over and scooped the cat up with one hand and the object up with the other. As soon as my fingers closed around it, I knew what it was. I'd used one many times in the past, and never for good reason.

It was the plastic cap to a syringe.

I whipped back around and studied the room again. This time, I caught all the sinister nuances that told me something was wrong: the stool shoved away from the foot of the bed, the muddy bootprint near the balcony door. The faint scent of vomit hung in the air, and a patch of the wood floor was shiny, as if someone had hastily tried to clean it.

The pieces snapped together in one horrifying puzzle. Phil was in trouble.

Guilt mangled with rage flashed through me. The cat mewed pitifully, and this time, I agreed with him. I knew we shouldn't have stayed the night.

I dropped the cat and ran for the stairs. I burst into the courtyard and heard talking and clattering dishes coming from the veranda that overlooked the canal. Most of the family was already gathered around the long table, gossiping over bowls of rice porridge. I brushed past them and shoved my way into the kitchen.

Lanzhou, Bowen, and several others bustled about the cramped space. Lanzhou stood over one of the giant iron woks that was inlaid in the vintage brick stove. *"Zǎo!"* he greeted me warmly.

I forwent all the rules of etiquette. "Has anyone seen Philadelphia?"

The chatter ceased as everyone turned to look at me. Their stunned silence gave me the answer I needed.

Lanzhou dropped his *chuan*. "What's wrong?"

I held the syringe cap out to him. "What did you do to her?"

Lanzhou had the decency to look horrified, but Bowen wasted no time in going on the defensive. "What do you mean, 'what did we do to her'? Where is she?"

"That's what I'd like to know," I shot back. "She's gone, and it looks like there's been a break-in."

Lanzhou turned and called to his nephew, who was standing across the kitchen. "I want a perimeter check, now. Search the entire house. Send someone down to the square and make sure she's not there."

The young man darted off to obey.

Bowen couldn't muster the energy to be worried. "Are we sure she didn't just wander off? She's a teenager."

"Of course, she didn't just 'wander off.'" I mocked him with air quotes. "First, she's too terrified to go anywhere without me. Second, she didn't take her phone."

Bowen shrugged. "She doesn't need it if she's not planning on checking in online. Maybe she just needed some time away from you."

"He's right." Lanzhou physically put himself between us, which was probably the only thing that stopped me from punching Bowen in the nose. "Let's not lose our heads just yet. She might have just gone to the—"

"Don't argue with me about Philadelphia!" I yelled. "I know her better than all of you put together. She would not leave without me. Go check the room if you want, but I'm telling you, she's in trouble, and I want answers."

Bowen correctly assumed that the accusation in my voice was aimed at him. "What makes you think we know anything?"

"She's *your* Blue Fire," I threatened. "You're supposed to be protecting her."

Lanzhou laid a warning hand on my arm, but it did nothing to ground me. "We had guards posted outside the house all night," he said, voice deliberately calm. He turned to Bowen. "Did they say anything when you relieved them this morning?"

Bowen shook his head. "Nothing to report."

"Unless they were bribed," I hissed.

Bowen's gaze darkened. "Exactly what are you suggesting?"

Lanzhou pinched me, but I shrugged him off. "Exactly what you think I'm suggesting."

Bowen's biceps tensed. "Why would we kidnap her? She's one of us."

She *wasn't* one of them, but he had a point. They had no reason to kidnap her while she was sleeping under their roof—unless they'd overheard our argument last night and knew we would be leaving.

But even then, threatening her would have been inefficient. She wasn't the unknown in this equation; I was. If they wanted to convince Phil to stay on Earth and lead the revolution, I was the one they needed to get out of the way.

As if sensing my thoughts, Bowen turned the interrogation back on me. "What about you? Your room was close to hers. Did you hear anything last night?"

"No…" I didn't even finish the thought before I realized my mistake. I hadn't heard anything last night. I'd put my headphones in so I wouldn't have to listen to her cry—never realizing that was when she would need me the most.

I spun towards the door. "I'm going to find her."

"Nic, stop." Lanzhou blocked my path. "If she really is in trouble, we're going to need help. Let us search the house, talk to the guards who were on shift last night. If we can't find her, we'll send out a search party."

Bowen finally decided to take the situation seriously. "I'll call them right now." He strode out of the room.

I appreciated that he was making himself useful, but I wasn't going to wait around while they ran through their petty due process. "We don't have time for this! She's the most wanted woman on Earth right now."

"Who do you think might have taken her?" Lanzhou asked. "Think. Is there anyone I should know about?"

I shook my head; I had absolutely no idea who would want to kidnap her. Bowen was right; it probably wasn't one of them. And it definitely wasn't Asia; she would have just burned the whole house down. Asia was not one to be subtle, and she had no reason to work secretly in the dark. If the government had found Phil, they would have taken both of us and raided the entire house while they were at it.

No, process of elimination suggested that whoever had kidnapped her was acting outside the rule of both the United and the underground. They answered to no one, which meant they had no incentive to keep her in once piece. Whatever their plan was, they would not be kind to her.

The realization filled me with such anger and dread that I almost wished it *was* Asia who had taken her. At least I could trust Asia to be civil.

Lanzhou steadied me with a hand to the shoulder. "You need to sit down."

That was the exact opposite of what I should be doing. "No, I'm going to look for her." I tried to shove past him.

Lanzhou sighed and pushed me back. "Nic, seriously, think this through. What are you going to do? Start going door to door? You don't even have a functioning phone."

He was right, and that just made me hate myself even more. Not that I needed any help in that department.

"Look, I promise we will find her. You have the entire underground on your side. I just talked to Jael's people—they'll be here any minute. She can help; she's got access to the algorithm."

"Good for her, but that won't help us. Phil doesn't have any electronics on her."

"No, but whoever took her might. Please, just wait for Jael. We'll figure this out together."

I grunted my consent. Jael was the last person I wanted to involve, but if she truly was as powerful as everyone said, then she was Phil's best bet. I certainly didn't have any better ideas.

Lanzhou took advantage of my silence to shove a bowl of porridge into my hand. "Sit, eat something. I'll go get the rest of the family together."

He pushed me out of the kitchen and steered me towards the now-vacant table on the veranda. I unwillingly slumped down on the bench. After waiting to make sure I was going to stay put, Lanzhou took off, shouting across the courtyard in Mandarin.

I glared at the soupy contents of my bowl. I had no desire to eat any of it, but I didn't have anything better to do. Lanzhou was right; there was nothing I could do. I couldn't get online, I couldn't track her, and I didn't know anything about the area. I hadn't been this useless since Phil and I were trapped in Wing 74.

Abruptly, I remembered watching her final stream and hearing the gunshot and the shriek as the camera went black—and realizing that she'd just sacrificed herself to save everyone. She'd risked her life to do what was right after my choices had put her in danger. Again.

I roared and hurled my bowl onto the deck. The porcelain shattered with a crash as hot rice splattered up my leg. I welcomed the brief flash of pain.

A gasp came from behind me. "Whoa, dude, wasting food is not cool."

I froze. I knew that voice. *Dear God, anyone but them.*

Unsurprisingly, God wasn't interested in granting my sacrilegious requests. A second voice joined the conversation. "Yeah, I would have eaten that!"

Yup, there was the other one. I begrudgingly turned around.

It was John and Dowe.

16: PHILADELPHIA

The world was still spinning when I came to.

The first thing I registered was a nauseous wave of dizziness, that endless swirling that told me I'd be better off asleep than awake. I tried to push past it, searching for solid ground, any feeling I could grab and center my senses on. I opened my eyes, but all I could see was darkness and flashing colors that I wasn't sure were real or imagined. I tried to speak but couldn't; my breath caught on something painful and sticky, jamming the air in my throat. I tried to move my hands but couldn't do that either; sharp metal bit into my wrists, and my back was pressed against something cold. I twisted but nothing budged, I screamed but no sound came out, and all the while the colors in the room were burning brighter and brighter until I could practically hear them ringing in my ears.

Jesus, Jesus, Jesus...

Breathe. Breathe.

I pinched my eyes shut again. I forced myself to hold still and start praying. The words were nonsense, but I repeated them over and over until I reconnected with the feeling that I wasn't alone in the world. I waited until I could count to three between each breath, then opened my eyes again.

I took stock of my senses—slowly this time. I was sitting on a soggy dirt floor in a dark room. My hands were cuffed behind my back, and I felt a metal pole between my shoulder blades. A thick piece of tape was slapped over my mouth, pulling on loose hairs that had fallen out of my ponytail. And everything—*everything*—hurt.

I struggled to swallow my heart as a blanket of fear dropped over me. I was no stranger to fear; I'd stared down guns, fallen from great heights, and danced with death more than once. But this was different. This wasn't the jolt of terrified energy that shot through me when my flight-or-flight response kicked in. This was slow and heavy, a weight that settled in my lungs like the oxygen had gotten sucked out of the room. This was a dread, the realization that something very bad was about to happen.

And I could do nothing to stop it.

Holy Spirit, I need you now.

I didn't feel any peace, but I banked on the trust that He was there. I looked around and tried to figure out where I was. As my eyes adjusted to the darkness, I could tell I was in a small room. All the windows were boarded up, so the only light came from holes and gaps in the wood. There were heaps of trash piled against the walls, making me wonder if the garbage was the only thing keeping the house from caving in. The whole place smelled rancid and musty, like the dirt floor never fully dried in between rains.

I twisted and looked behind me. I was cuffed to the frame of what had, at some point, been a bunk bed. So many of the crossbars were broken or missing that you probably couldn't have put a mattress on it even if you wanted to, but it was still heavy enough that I had no hope of dragging it.

Before I could formulate any more questions, noise erupted outside. Gruff comments were exchanged, and then the gap of light underneath the door was blocked out. I sat up straight and summoned all my defenses as a key rattled in the lock. The door swung open, revealing a flood of morning light and the silhouette of a man.

He stood there, staring, waiting until my vision adjusted to the light and I could focus on his face.

Jayde.

Suddenly, all my questions were answered. I knew exactly what was going on. In spite of myself, I began to tremble as I accepted the inevitable.

Jayde was going to kill me. The only wonder why he hadn't done it already.

He kicked the door mostly shut, leaving a shaft of light just barely enough to see by. He squatted next to me and studied me, arms propped on his knees. I searched his face for any emotion, but there was none, not even anger. He was calm, controlled. He looked just like he did any other day, like this was a regular staff meeting in the office.

He reached up and grabbed the back of my head. I shuddered as his calloused fingers brushed my neck. He used his other hand to rip the gag off in one sharp yank. I gasped for air as my eyes watered and my face burned.

He wadded the tape up and tossed it across the room. He seemed content with the silence, as if waiting for me to speak first. I had nothing to say and absolutely no desire to talk to him.

He finally got bored of waiting. "No questions?"

I took a deep breath. If he was going to make me talk, I might as well get some information. "How'd you find me?" I ventured, and winced when I realized how dry and cracked my voice was. I swallowed fruitlessly.

He gave a hollow laugh. "I didn't have to 'find' you, Phil. The entire Chinese underground knows you were at church. I have a friend who works at that factory. He volunteered to be on guard at the house last night."

I clenched my fists behind my back. This was why Nic hadn't wanted me to reveal myself. As always, he'd been right— right about everything.

"And I suppose you're here to finish the job," I returned.

He snorted. "I wish."

I felt annoyance flare up in me. All my adrenaline was tired of cycling around my nerves with nowhere to go. "Just get it over with. If you think I'm going to beg and plead, you'll be disappointed. I'm not bargaining with you."

The bravado in my voice was weak, but the threat was real. He'd get nothing from me.

He shook his head. "Sounds fun, but not today. We've got other business to attend to."

Suddenly, my panic found something to focus on, and a fresh wave of terror washed over me. "What?"

He fingered his holstered gun. "Look, you have no idea how much I'd love to kill you right now…"

I have an inkling, I thought but wasn't dumb enough to say.

"But thankfully for you, a mutual friend has convinced me that you're still worth more alive than dead."

"Who?" Who was Jayde talking to that would argue for my life? Only a handful of people knew Jayde and I were in Beijing. Was it my uncle? My uncle Tower had known about the assassination; surely, he would fight for me, if he knew what was happening. But would Jayde tell him what was going on?

Jayde wasn't forthcoming with the information. "Since Operation Thunderbird was conveniently top secret, there are only a handful of people who know you failed. As far as the rest of the underground knows, you're just hiding out waiting for stuff to blow over. All you have to do is record a video saying you're back in command, and this all goes away. You go back to being the pretty face of the revolution, and Operation Blue Fire continues as scheduled."

That explained a lot. Jayde was still planning to launch a revolution, and he wanted me to lead. I was still his Blue Fire— except he didn't realize that he wasn't in charge anymore.

"It won't work," I challenged. "They won't listen to you. They're loyal to me."

Unfortunately, this was not news to him. "Oh yes, I know all about Lev's little mutiny." The slithering tone of his voice made my blood run cold. "But this isn't a numbers game, princess. It doesn't matter whether they're loyal to me or not. Whoever controls the thunderbird controls the war."

You don't control me. I shoved him away with my foot. "I'm not recording anything for you."

He hit me. Drew his arm back and slapped me across the face. I gasped as the room spun like a kaleidoscope.

"If I have to cuff you to a chair in front of a camera, I will," he declared. His voice was steady, almost bored, as if he'd rehearsed this whole exchange. "But I'm sure we can come to an agreement. You're easy to motivate."

I had been—once. But his collateral, Stanyard, was safely out of reach. There was no one else he could threaten—

He spoke before I finished the thought. "I still have your father."

"But he's gone," I argued, before realizing I was playing right into his hand. My father was alive, and according to Stanyard, he was doing well physically. But he had lost all his memories; he didn't even know me.

"If that mattered to you, you never would have thawed him out." Jayde read my mind. "But you're right, threatening to kill him is a bit passé. It would be much more fun to play with his memories. Perhaps, give him some new ones—about you."

Is that possible? I thought but daren't ask. I tried to deflect the panic; there was no way Mrs. Nolan, Thames's wife, would let Jayde touch my father. She was supervising my father's therapy and had promised to keep him safe until I returned—but if Jayde had enough people on his side, there might not be anything she could do to stop him.

As if that wasn't threatening enough, Jayde autofilled several other insidious possibilities. "Or, if that doesn't work, I know where your brother is. Or the Vons. You're such a kind, caring person, Philadelphia Smyrna—you give me so much material to work with."

I won't do it. The determination formed in my mind, but I couldn't find the words. I wouldn't—would I? We'd been through this whole song and dance before. I knew what could happen if I ignored the Lord and compromised instead of trusting Him to protect the ones I loved. I wouldn't make the same mistake, not this time.

Except, I still wasn't convinced that leading the revolution *was* a mistake.

Jayde didn't wait for me to find my moral compass. "You think about it and let me know whose life you'd like to play with. But in the meantime, as far as anyone else knows, you never went to Beijing, there was no Operation Thunderbird, and we're still the best of friends—got it?"

"And how do you want me to explain the bruise you just gave me?" I snarled.

He drew his hand back like he was going to give me another one. I pinched my eyes shut and braced myself. *Jesus, help.*

After a moment's hesitation, Jayde grunted. "You're right, I'd better not mess up that pretty face of yours. There's only so much makeup can fix."

I opened my eyes and waited.

"We leave for Boston in a few hours. In the meantime, I *don't* trust you to sit still, so hopefully this helps."

Jayde pulled a roll of duct tape from the pocket of his cargo pants and tore off a generous strip. The hideous sound of the tape unwinding sent my panic into overdrive. I barely managed to swallow a cry of pain as Jayde grabbed my chin and gagged me with more force than was necessary.

Holy Spirit, please don't leave me.

Jayde rose and walked to the door. I tried to look past him as he opened it, but all I could see was what looked like a stone courtyard and a few more guards.

Jayde hesitated in the doorway with his back to me. "Do you know why I hate you so much, Phil?"

I didn't particularly want to know, but he volunteered the answer. "Because you have what so many people have *died* trying to get, and you're willing to throw it all away."

He looked back at me. When he spoke, his voice was quiet, transparent—almost like we were equal partners again. "Hundreds of people have tried over the years to start a revolution or change the law—and they've all failed. They've all been killed or swept under the rug, and the United only got more powerful. Then you come along, and suddenly, you have an entire army following you. Overnight you've managed to create an entire freedom movement—do you understand how improbable that is?"

I did. I would have called it a miracle, because it was one.

Even if Nic didn't think so.

Jayde's calm demeanor broke. I couldn't read his facial expression against the backlight of the morning sun, but I could hear the emotion in his voice. He sounded confused. Sad. In pain. "I still don't know how you did it. I don't know what it is about you that everyone loves. But you have *everything*—you, and only you, can do this. You could save the world. But you won't."

He took a deep breath, and I saw the anger returning to his posture. "I'll never understand you," he muttered, and punctuated with some foul terms. "But we're going to do this whether you like it or not. So the choice is yours: You can be an army general, or you can be a prisoner of war. Hopefully, a little more time locked in here will help you decide which one."

Then he slammed and latched the door, leaving me with that final threat.

I waited until the voices had faded outside before putting my face to my knees. My head spun, but this time, it wasn't because I was dizzy. No, my mind was reeling because I knew Jayde was right.

I did have everything—but it wasn't because I was anyone special. All I'd done was help Nic destroy a factory of Red Rain. That video had leaked to the internet, where it had trended instantly. Thames had added fuel to the fire by forcing me to record more videos recounting my life story, but I knew he wasn't responsible for making me the figurehead of a revolution. Only one person could be responsible for that.

God.

No matter what Nic said, I genuinely believed God had turned me into Blue Fire. Maybe Nic was right about some things; maybe Asia had invited me to the party because she wanted me to kill her father. Maybe she was using my image to start her own war. But that still didn't explain why my videos had trended in the first place. Even Asia herself admitted she had nothing to do with that. And if that wasn't God, then who was it? If God didn't want me to change the world, then why was I here?

And I still believed in the rebellion, didn't I? Jayde was a monster, and I wanted nothing to do with him—but revolution was the right thing to do, wasn't it? I still believed the United was evil. I still wanted to save the unassimilated and rescue everyone who had suffered in a containment camp like I did. I still intended to fight for freedom. I was still Blue Fire—even if I wasn't the Blue Fire Jayde wanted me to be.

But could there be a revolution as long as Jayde was involved? I didn't trust him; frankly, I didn't trust most of the underground. And maybe that was the real problem: Even if Operation Blue Fire did succeed, who would end up on top? Would the new world be any better than the last?

It wouldn't be if people like Jayde were in charge. Jayde had proven he was willing to sacrifice all morals to win. I had no doubt that he'd apply the same logic to a reformed government, whatever that might look like.

No, the more I learned about Jayde and the underground, the more I was convinced that the rebels couldn't be trusted with the government any more than the Beijing leadership could. My chest tightened when I realized that's what Nic had been trying to tell me all along. That's why he'd wanted me to come home.

Had he been right? Were we supposed to run back to Mars and hide—until what? Until the perfect leader came along? The perfect leader didn't exist. There was no such thing as the perfect opportunity, the perfect government, the perfect moment in time. Unless Jesus came back tomorrow, there was no way to reform the world overnight. No matter who did it or how it happened, change would be a slow process. A slow, painful, potentially bloody process.

Was I still the person God had called to start that change? Or was Nic right? What if God didn't call me at all? What if I really hadn't heard from the Lord?

I searched for an answer, but there was none. If I blocked out the rattle of fear, I could sense the Holy Spirit nearby, like He was sitting in the room with me. But He was eerily silent. I felt no unction, no wisdom, no push in any direction. It felt like *none* of the options were right—which led me to suspect that none of them were.

I twisted my wrists and felt the jade bangle slide on my arm. I hoped that lady had been telling the truth when she said the church was praying for me, because right now, I didn't have any other options. I'd been able to blast my way out of a lot of prisons, but Jayde had been smart this time. I groaned and tried to shift my position, but I just succeeded in pinching my skin in the cuffs. I winced as the will to cry shoved to the forefront of my mind. I wasn't going anywhere—and Nic, the one person who could possibly rescue me, had no idea where I was.

I trusted that Nic knew me well enough to realize I didn't just run off. He would know something was wrong, but he had no way of knowing Jayde was involved. There was no way to track me; I didn't have any electronics that would give away my position. No, by the time Nic had any inkling of what was going on, Jayde and I would be back in Boston.

And then, if Jayde had his way, even Asia wouldn't be able to find me.

17: NIC

"Man, are we happy to see you, Q!"

The feeling was not mutual. I stood up and backed away so I could study the pair from a safe distance. John and Dowe had been my prison mates on Rott, and like everything else from my time in jail, I would have preferred to leave them in the past.

It wasn't that they were terrible people; in fact, they met all the criteria to be classified as friends. But while they had been valuable allies, their personalities seemed uniquely designed to torment me. They had no social skills, no shame, and no concept of an "indoor voice." They were also obnoxious to look at; they were so very nearly identical that it looked like God had gone CTRL+C, CTRL+V. And yet, as far as I was aware, they weren't related—not that I'd wasted much brain power trying to unravel the mystery that was John and Dowe.

I certainly didn't have any mental energy to deal with them today. "What are you doing here?" I demanded in a way that I hoped came off as unwelcoming.

They were not deterred. "We're here to see you! Why else would we come to Beijing?" Dowe replied.

"Yeah!" John echoed. "We came as soon as we heard Blue Fire was here!"

"Wait." I put up my hand to pause the conversation while I did the math. "How did you get here?"

"Same way we always get to China," Dowe deadpanned.

"No, I mean, a flight to China takes at least thirteen hours. We just checked in last night. How'd you get here so fast?"

John looked like he was prepared to mouth off, then hesitated. He turned to Dowe. "How *did* we get here so fast?"

Dowe looked as astounded as the rest of us. "You're right, by all accounts it doesn't make sense."

"John, Dowe, you made it!" Lanzhou darted onto the veranda. "It's so great to see you. Welcome back." He offered them both a hug and a slap on the back, which they reciprocated with far too much enthusiasm.

"You know these guys?" I exclaimed.

"Doesn't everybody know a John Dowe?" Lanzhou returned with a wink. He turned to me. "Sorry to break up the reunion…"

"No, please do," I groaned.

Lanzhou ignored the comment. "I've got Jael on the line in the other room. She wants to speak with you."

Finally, we can make some real progress. I nodded at Lanzhou to lead the way, then followed him across the courtyard to his father's study. John and Dowe scampered behind like lost puppies.

Bowen and the rest of the family were already crammed around the massive desk, talking to someone on the computer. They cleared the way so I could stand in front of the monitor.

A black woman about my age was on the screen. Everything about her could be described as *imposing*, from her fierce glare to the wildly embroidered turban that was wrapped around her head like a crown. She certainly carried herself like a queen; she sat up straight and looked down at the camera at a slight angle, as if we were all subjects in her courtroom.

"Q," she said, dipping her head in greeting. "Pleased to make your acquaintance." Her voice was seasoned with a rich Hausa accent, which somehow made her sound all the more imperial.

"The pleasure is all mine, I'm sure," I returned. "Your reputation precedes you."

She arched one cat-like eyebrow. "I shall endeavor to live up to it. I'm sorry I can't be there in person, but my flight won't land for another three hours."

As if corroborating her statement, her camera jolted, like her plane was going through turbulence. *At least someone has to obey the laws of physics.*

"Amateur," Dowe smirked, loud enough for everyone to hear.

Jael wasn't having it. Her entire demeanor changed. "John. Dowe. Front and center. *Now.*"

They elbowed their way up to the desk, which put them much too close to me. Jael drew herself up higher until her forehead was grazing the top of the frame. "Do not backtalk me," she ordered. "The whole reason Blue Fire is in this mess is because you failed the mission. If she gets hurt, I *will* court martial you."

There were several important pieces of information in that sentence, and I tried to quickly sort them by relevance. "Mission?"

"Yeah!" John squealed like it was bring-your-kid-to-work day. "That's our boss!"

I wasn't sure whether that doubled or halved my respect for the woman. "I am so sorry," I said, looking back at the screen.

She dipped her head. "Thank you for your condolences."

"And what, exactly, was this mission, and how does it involve Philadelphia?" I continued before John or Dowe could mouth off.

"Doctor, I've known about 'Operation Thunderbird' the whole time," Jael said, voice dripping with patronizing benevolence. "Tower has been in contact with me."

I paused while my brain categorized that data. "Well, at least he's not a total deadbeat of an uncle."

Jael almost smiled. "I had intended to intercept Blue Fire before she got to the General. Unfortunately, my agents missed the date." Her voice hardened over with accusation.

John paled. "The birthday party's *today*?"

"It was Saturday," Jael deadpanned.

"Wait, you were supposed to be there?" I yelled. "And you *forgot the date*?" I wasn't sure which I found more shocking: The fact that someone else had tried to save Phil, or the fact that they'd failed because they couldn't keep a calendar.

Dowe shrugged sheepishly. "I could've sworn Andi said it was July 4th…"

"That was three weeks ago," Lanzhou pointed out.

"So?" Dowe frowned, as if going back in time was something he had been planning to do all along.

John was still panicking. "I left my gift at home…"

I slapped my hands down on the wooden desk. "Would someone other than John and Dowe like to explain what's going on?"

"I promise all your questions will be answered, doctor," Jael insisted, which sounded weirdly like a threat. "But at the moment, it sounds like we have a more immediate crisis. Lanzhou?"

He leaned over my shoulder so she could see him. "Blue Fire is gone, and I agree with Nic—it looks like foul play. We've searched the house and the square, but there's no sign of her."

"The guard who was on duty last night is conveniently not answering my calls," Bowen added, and had the decency to look ashamed.

"Well, luckily for us all, his phone is still online—which tells me everything I need to know." Jael paused for unnecessary drama. "Jayde has our Blue Fire."

John and Dowe gasped in unison, supplying the disgust I was too tired to express. That little revelation answered all my questions and confirmed my worst fears. Of all the people who wanted to hurt Philadelphia, Jayde would be the cruelest.

"Well, you'd better hope she's not dead already," I snapped.

"She's not," Jael declared with a confidence that came off as heartless. "I have every reason to believe that Jayde needs Blue Fire alive as much as the rest of us do."

I did not appreciate the content of her sentence or the attitude she used to punctuate it. "What do you mean?"

The rings on her fingers flashed as she flicked her hand across the screen. "Jayde's recent texts and calls make it very clear he's still planning to launch a revolution, and for that, he needs a living thunderbird."

That's what I'm afraid of. "And how do you know he has her?" I challenged.

"I've been tracking his cell phone activity." She sounded almost bored by the question, as if I ought to have known the answer already. "For the past few days, he's been trailing you two. Every time you checked in, he showed up to the same place a few hours later. And last night, he was at the house, along with several of his friends. His phone registered on the Tangs' router."

I gripped the edge of the desk as rage rolled through me. Jayde had simply waltzed in and snatched Philadelphia right off her balcony—all the while I'd been just a few doors away, lost in my own conceit.

Lanzhou spoke before I could get too invested in self-laceration. "And who is this Jayde, exactly?"

"You may know him as the Green Dragon," Jael explained. "He's, shall we say, a former friend of Philadelphia's from Boston."

Lanzhou glanced at me. "So when you say you had a mission go awry..."

"I'll debrief you later," Jael interrupted. "For now, our focus is getting Philadelphia back before Jayde tries to leave the city. I attempted to reach out and *introduce* myself," she stretched the word into a threat, "but he's not returning my calls. So we'll have to do this the hard way."

I took a deep breath and stuffed my emotions back in the closet. "And that is?"

"Jayde's cell phone activity puts him in a neighborhood across town. He's been there since late last night. If Philadelphia is still alive, she's there. We're going to go get her out."

I straightened. "Excellent. When do we leave?"

"Immediately." Jael straightened, and her voice took on a militaristic edge. "Lanzhou, you're in charge of this mission."

At least that was a decision I could agree with. "I'm with him," I declared, and was somewhat surprised when no one argued.

Jael nodded. "Bowen, you too. I want four more."

"Us!" John and Dowe shrieked in unison.

"No," I snapped.

"Yes," Jael countered me. "This is their mission, and they're going to finish it."

I had several follow-up arguments—the primary one being that Phil was in this mess partially because of John and Dowe's earlier failure. But Jael continued barking orders before I could voice my concerns. "I need two more volunteers."

"I can pull some men off the line at the factory," Bowen offered. "They can get here in fifteen minutes."

"Perfect," Jael agreed.

I added the numbers. "Only seven?"

"Any more, and we'll likely attract attention moving in a pack," Lanzhou explained.

That was a fair point, but it didn't inspire confidence. "You'd better hope Jayde doesn't have more than six friends with him," I muttered.

"He doesn't, not according to the cellular traffic in that area." The glare of a backlit screen flickered across Jael's face, like she was verifying her findings as she talked. "I've analyzed all the registered devices that have connected to that cell tower in the last twelve hours. Of them, only a handful are people I suspect are associated with Jayde. Of course, the algorithm isn't perfect, but it's a risk we're going to have to take if we want to be discreet. I'd like to avoid getting the real police involved if possible."

"Don't have to tell me twice," I muttered, but cast a wary glance at John and Dowe.

"I'd also like to avoid causing a commotion in the underground until I know what Jayde is planning." Jael swiveled her eyes in a firm, nonnegotiable glare that seemed to include everyone in the room, even though she was confined to the monitor. "The operation is hanging by a thread as it is. If we can keep this *indiscretion* between us, I may still be able to reason with Jayde without causing factions. So I want weapons set on stun, and we're not taking any prisoners—am I understood?"

I grunted. I couldn't care less about Jayde's feelings, and the entire revolution could crash and burn for all I cared. If I got a shot at that monster, I was taking it.

"That includes you, doctor."

I looked up to find Jael arching her eyebrows. It was a patronizing stare, like she knew she was in control of the entire situation even though she was however-many miles away.

I folded my arms. I wasn't about to apologize for my protectiveness of Phil.

"Unless..." She shifted back from the camera, as if my very existence was beneath her. "You'd like to stay home while my team does the rescuing."

I looked at the dozen family members gathered around me. There was an audible shift in the room, and Lanzhou pinched my arm warningly. Even Dowe shook his head at me, and he was not subtle about it.

I didn't care want any of them thought, but I was one man against ten. Worse, I was the outsider here. The Tangs might know my father, but they were more loyal to Jael than me. I wasn't about to try my luck with those odds.

I unzipped my jacket and made a dramatic scene of pulling out my gun and changing the setting. I jammed it back in its holster and deferred to Jael with a mocking bow.

She smirked, revealing the tiniest sliver of her white teeth that stood out like diamonds on her dark face. "Let's move out."

*

Jayde's current location put him at the heart of the city, which meant rush hour was our greatest enemy. Public transportation was out of the question, and it would take hours for us to crawl through the standstill on the highway.

Thankfully, Bowen had a solution: motorbikes. I hadn't ridden one since college, but muscle memory kicked in after a few wobbly laps around the alley. I wasn't about to buddy ride with someone else, even though John graciously offered.

After suiting up with helmets and an ample amount of weapons, we headed out. Lanzhou led the way, following the directions Jael sent him. We rode single file along the riverbank until we reached the end of the dock. Then Lanzhou led us on a twisted tour of the city, crisscrossing alleyways, cutting across courtyards, and skirting sidewalks in a way that was probably illegal. We reached our destination in thirty minutes, a herculean record for rush hour.

I could only hope we weren't thirty minutes too late.

The neighborhood Jael sent us to was definitely a slum. It was a *hutong*, a network of alleys created by interlocking courtyard homes. Several centuries ago, the brick structures would have represented the crown of old Beijing's culture and history. But the United had no taste for culture or history, and the neighborhood had been left to rot.

Several streets had been demolished and the debris left heaped along the road, the marker of a failed urban renewal project. Many of the remaining homes had been condemned and abandoned; their tile roofs were crumbling, exposing rotting beams. The seamless brick walls blended into a blur of tired gray, decorated only by irreverent graffiti.

But despite the stench of death that hung over the neighborhood, it was evident that people still lived there. Rusty bikes collapsed beside backdoors, while retrofitted window units struggled against the summer heat. Laundry hung from every awning, and a few food vendors struggled to eke out a living on the street corners. All the residents I saw looked as tired and worn down as the buildings themselves, like they were one breath away from collapsing.

We ditched the bikes on the outskirts of the neighborhood. Bowen bribed a wrinkled old man into letting us park in his courtyard and assigned one of the young men from the factory to guard them.

I yanked my helmet off and tossed it on the ground. "What now?" I hissed to Lanzhou, and hoped the homeowner didn't understand much English.

"We split up, two and two. Jayde is still in the neighborhood—Jael says he made a call two minutes ago." Lanzhou scrolled on his device.

"And she can't give us a more precise pinpoint?"

Lanzhou shrugged. "He's on cellular data—all she has is the general area."

I groaned. Where was the surveillance state when you needed it?

Lanzhou tried to comfort me with a pat on the arm, which had the opposite effect on my nerves. "I promise she's still here. Jayde won't leave without her. So either we'll find her, or we'll find Jayde."

He turned to the rest of the team. "We'll start at the west end and work our way east. Check every abandoned building, ask the residents if they saw anything suspicious last night."

I doubted anyone had seen anything; that's why Jayde had chosen this neighborhood as a hideout. It was a sketchy part of town. No one would question a suspicious vehicle or a couple of thugs passing through.

"If you find anything, radio." Bowen passed a walkie talkie to each member of the group. "Don't go in alone."

The latter admonition was directed at me. I glared at him as I snatched the radio from his hand.

"And remember, keep it down!" Dowe urged in a voice that was the exact opposite of quiet.

"Be discreet. Blend with the surroundings," John added.

If we wanted to be discreet, we shouldn't have brought you, I thought. Dowe looked normal enough, but John wore a bulky parka that was completely inappropriate for the season. His pockets were clearly loaded with contraband; his jacket was so lumpy that he looked like a stupid inflatable at a used car lot. We'd be lucky if he didn't get reported as a "suspicious package."

As if hearing my thoughts and deciding to punish me for them, Lanzhou announced, "Nic and John, you're together."

"What?" we both screeched at the same time.

"I wanted to go with Dowe," John pouted.

Wow, rejected by John. This was a new low in my life.

"Don't shoot the messenger, these are Jael's assignments." Lanzhou shrugged, but even he was frowning at his phone skeptically. "Dowe, you're with me. Bowen, take Haoyu. Let's roll!"

We split up, each team taking a street. I ran down the block and hoped John would keep up. I didn't even bother to look at the first few buildings; this end of the neighborhood was too busy, with several stores and a bus stop. There was no way Jayde could hide here.

John huffed and panted from behind me. "Whoa, Q, aren't you going to stop and look for evidence?"

I wasn't about to waste time explaining my logic to him. I kept running, scanning the shuttered buildings for anything out of the ordinary. But in truth, I had no idea what I was looking for. The neighborhood was huge, and we were dealing with a semi-professional. Jayde wasn't brilliant, but he wasn't sloppy. He would have covered his tracks. And meanwhile, the locals were already giving us—well, mostly John—suspicious looks. If we wanted to stay under the radar, banging down doors and asking people if they'd seen a red-haired military brat seemed ill-advised.

I halted in the middle of the road and let the wave of hopelessness catch up to me. We would never find her in here, and if we created too big of a stir, Jayde would bail—or just shoot Philadelphia to bury the evidence.

It took John a full thirty seconds to reach me. He staggered and braced himself against the nearest wall. "How... do..." He gulped in air and tried again. "How do... you live this way? Whew..."

"What do you mean?" I asked, not that I really cared.

"All this running."

As often was the case with John and Dowe, it was a strangely metaphorical statement. I hated it when they waxed philosophical.

"One sec, I'm almost ready." John raised one finger, took a deep breath, and meowed.

I jerked back. Even he looked surprised by the sound that had come from his lips. He cleared his throat and opened his mouth to try again. There was another mew—but this time, I could clearly tell it was coming from inside his jacket.

My mathematical brain instantly put two and two together. "You didn't."

John turned red all the way up to the edge of his receding hairline. "How could I say no? He was begging to come with..."

He unzipped his jacket, and that stupid cat popped his head out. John reached down and scratched behind the cat's ears. "Besides, he's *so cute.*"

That was the last word I would have used to describe the animal. I groaned and pinched my temples. "Look, John, I appreciate that you're trying to help..." I patronized him, even though neither half of that statement was true. "But I don't feel like you're grasping the severity of the situation. Need I remind you that Philadelphia could *die*?"

All of my frustration came out in a shout, which neither the cat nor John appreciated. John gasped, and the cat took off. He wiggled out of John's coat, clawed up on his shoulder, and jumped. He landed on the roof of the house behind us and started scampering along the edge.

"Come back, kitty!" John cried, standing on his toes and swiping at the animal. "Oh no, Phil's gonna kill me if I lose her cat…"

"Wait." I grabbed his arm and held him back. The cat paused at the end of the house and turned to look at me, glassy eyes blinking. Then he flicked his tail and kept moving.

Suddenly, I knew what to do. It was a dumb idea, spoken by a voice I hadn't talked to in years, but I decided to take the bait.

"You'd better not make me look like an idiot," I muttered aloud.

"Who are you talking to?" John asked.

"Not you," I intoned. I pointed. "We have to follow that stupid cat!"

John needed no encouragement and took off at a run.

We barreled down the alley, avoiding piles of trash and fallen bricks while we kept one eye on the cat. He slinked along the edge of the interconnected roofs, slipping under the power lines that hung dangerously low. He led us down a narrow passageway to the next street over and then back again, occasionally pausing on the corner to sniff the air.

Abruptly, he stopped in the middle of a roof. He climbed up to the peak and glanced back at me, whiskers twitching. Then he leapt over the edge and disappeared into the courtyard beyond.

"This has to be it—she's here." I scanned the alley. The house and the ones on either side of it were abandoned, the perfect place for a handful of criminals to hide out for the night. We were on the backside of the building, and the rear door and all the windows were boarded up.

"This way," John whispered. He squeezed into the narrow passageway between the two houses. I followed, squatting to make sure I stayed out of sight of the windows. John found a place where the courtyard wall sagged low because several rows of brick were missing. He jumped up on an abandoned barrel with an agility that belied his age and peered into the courtyard.

"It's him—there's Jayde."

I let out my breath and thanked the voice in my head—and that stupid cat. "How many people does he have with him?" I asked, making sure to keep my voice low.

John counted off on his fingers. "Three in the courtyard."

I reached inside my jacket and powered on my gun, then hesitated. I could easily take the three of them out from over the courtyard wall, but there could be more guarding the main gate. We had no way of knowing how many there were or what kind of backup they had. As much as I wanted to drop Jayde in his tracks, if we wanted to avoid causing a commotion, we'd be better off luring them away from the house and sneaking Phil out the back.

"We need a distraction," I thought aloud.

"Say less," John crowed.

"A *small* one," I added when I remembered who I was talking to.

He slid a can of silly string back inside his coat. "Killjoy."

"Radio the others—get them to meet you out front. We need to draw them away from the main gate." I pictured the layout of the neighborhood in my mind as the pieces of the plan fell into place. "I'll jump the wall and get Phil out. Tell Lanzhou to meet me in the alley—we'll take Phil out through the back and be gone before they return."

We'd be safe as long as we could get to the more populated streets. Jayde couldn't risk causing a scene any more than we could.

"Genius," John said, and went for a high-five that I ignored. He shrugged it off and continued down the passageway, whispering into his radio.

I took the spot he had vacated and scanned the courtyard. Only one of the halls was still standing. Two burly young men armed with military rifles blocked the doorway. They were mere yards away from me, well within range of my electric pistol.

Suddenly, Jayde strode into view. He strutted about the courtyard, looking like a rooster with his shock of red hair. He barked something to the guards at the door.

I pulled my gun out of its holster and leveled it. I had a clear shot right at Jayde's head. I put my finger on the setting button.

Just then, a shout, a crash, and a squawk came from the next street over. At least, *squawk* was the best way I could describe the sound; it sounded like a startled chicken. And since John and Dowe were involved, I knew better than to ask questions.

Someone yelled for Jayde. He swore and turned to one of the boys guarding the door. "Do *not* move. You, with me." He ran out the main entrance, taking two of the other soldiers with him. The third planted himself in front of the door to the north hall.

I licked my lips in glorious anticipation. At least I'd get to shoot *something* today.

I waited until the shouts and squawking had faded into the distance, then took aim and fired. The electric bullet sapped the breath from the kid's lungs, and he slumped over without a sound.

Holstering my gun, I scrambled over the wall and dropped into the courtyard. I grabbed the guard's rifle and slammed it against the mulberry tree, bending the barrel and rendering it temporarily unusable. Then I rolled his body over. I patted down his pockets until I found what I was looking for: a keyring.

The key to the door was easy to spot; it was just as old and tarnished as the house itself. After glancing to make sure Jayde and his cronies hadn't come back yet, I unlocked the deadbolt and threw the door open.

There she was, huddled in the dark amongst piles of trash like unwanted merchandise. She was cuffed to the rusted skeleton of a bunk bed and gagged with a piece of tape. She groaned and lifted her head when I opened the door. She blinked at me, squinting in the light.

"Philadelphia. It's me." I enunciated slowly, knowing I would be nothing more than an imposing silhouette thanks to the dramatic backlighting.

She instantly came alive, jerking upright and squealing in relief.

I knelt beside her. "Hang on. This is going to hurt." I braced her neck with one hand, then ripped the tape off before either of us could think twice about it.

She gasped for breath. "Nic!" she cried, and the elated terror in her voice was all the thanks I needed.

"Let's get you out of here." I shifted through the guard's keyring, searching for the key to the cuffs.

She patiently held still. "How did you find me?"

"Jayde's stupid and made himself easy to track." I tried a key and grunted when it didn't fit. "I also feel obliged to admit that your stupid cat helped."

As if on command, the dumb animal made his appearance. He flounced in the door, meowing and flicking his tail like I was an announcer who had just welcomed him on stage. He jumped in Phil's lap and rubbed up against her, purring.

"Tommy!" she shrieked, and sounded like she was about to cry.

I gave her a once-over. Her eyes were bloodshot, and there were scratches on her hands and knees. Most telling, however, was the fact that one side of her face was inflamed.

"Are you okay?" I asked, before realizing that was a stupid question to ask someone who had just been kidnapped. I narrowed the search parameters. "Did he hurt you?"

"H-he hit me," she stuttered, as if she wasn't sure how to quantify her pain. "But I'm fine."

That was a lie if there ever was one. After the fifth attempt, I found the right key, and the cuffs released. I hurled them across the room with a growl. *I never should have set my weapon to stun.*

Finally free, Phil scrambled up, grabbed me around the neck, and burst into tears. She buried her face in my shoulder and sobbed, her whole body shaking. I braced myself against the bedframe and tried to recalibrate. I couldn't decide which was worse: the feel of her cold fingers gripping my shirt, or the sound of her shattered cries in my ear.

I straightened and gingerly pried her arms off my neck. "Look, I know you've had a traumatic experience…" I set her on her feet an acceptable distance away. "But that is not an excuse to sneak a hug in."

I expected her to laugh, but she didn't. She blinked, like she was too shellshocked to process that sarcasm was an acceptable form of communication. "Okay," she mumbled. She wiped her eyes and just stood there, apparently having no idea what to do next.

I didn't either. I wished I could take it back, but that would involve me *initiating* a hug. And that was a line neither of us were ready to cross.

I decided to exit the stage by leading the way towards the door. "Well, come meet our new friends."

She scooped up the cat and stumbled after me. "Friends?" She said the word with the same amount of skepticism I usually used for the concept.

I glanced back at her. "I found Jael."

18: PHILADELPHIA

John and Dowe were the last people I was expecting to find waiting outside, but I was nonetheless thrilled to see them.

"Philli!" they shrieked in their accidental unison. They both rushed at me and crushed me in a group hug from both sides. Tommy howled and squirmed out of my arms. I was so grateful for the physical reassurance that I almost started crying again.

Dowe soon got bored and let go, but John seemed to sense my need for comfort and stayed. He held me gently, standing firm and tall like my father used to, while I sniffled into his shoulder. "It's okay, Philli," he whispered, voice deep and clear. "You're safe now."

"Not yet she isn't," Nic barked. "We need to get out of here."

I tensed as the feeling of cold dread returned. *If Jayde catches me again...*

Dowe interrupted before my thoughts could reach their dark conclusion. "Yeah, those chickens won't distract them forever," he agreed.

I pulled away from John. "Chickens?"

He looked downright ashamed. "Don't ask—let's go!"

We ran to a place where the courtyard wall was broken down. I saw Lanzhou on the other side, waving at us. "This way!"

Dowe gave me a boost, and Lanzhou helped me down the other side. Tommy followed on his own, clearing the wall in one leap. Bowen and a young man I didn't recognize met us in the alley. Without a word, we headed west, Tommy trailing on Nic's ankles.

I kept glancing behind us as we ran. Lanzhou touched my shoulder. "Don't worry about Jayde. He won't try anything in public."

I struggled to believe him and stayed close to Nic.

We slowed when we reached the populated part of the neighborhood. We collected the motorbikes from an elderly gentleman who gave me a sideways glance but tactfully said nothing. Both John and Dowe tried to convince me to ride with them, but Nic overruled them with a stoney glare. I let John carry Tommy in his jacket as a compromise.

As soon as we got back to the house, the family took over. I was showered, fed, and checked over by a man who probably actually was a doctor. He declared me fine except for some scratches, gave me a handful of pills, and told me to rest.

While my aching joints longed to obey him, I realized as soon as I got upstairs that sleeping would be easier said than done. I pushed open the door to my bedroom and was instantly assaulted with a wave of cruel memories. The room felt dark and claustrophobic, even though it was blindingly lit with the noonday sun. I shut and latched all the windows and dragged the stool in front of the door to the hall, but I couldn't shake the feeling of being watched.

"It's fine," I coached myself aloud, suddenly afraid of the silence. "It's the middle of the day, and there's a dozen people in the house."

There were a dozen people in the house last night, too. I backed up and hit the bedframe. The feel of the pole between my shoulder blades reminded me of a dozen other painful senses: the sharp cuffs bruising my wrists, the sticky tape suffocating my cries for help, Jayde's hand hitting—

Something rustled behind me. I shrieked and whipped around, then let out my breath. It was just my cat lying in the middle of the bed. He meowed and rolled over, stretching out his belly as if tempting me to join him.

I forced myself to sit down next to him. "Are you trying to help?" Sinking back on the pile of pillows, I gathered him into my arms and was somewhat surprised when he didn't complain. I pressed his furry body to my chin and closed my eyes, focusing on the steady rumble of his contented purr.

"I need You," I whispered aloud. I wasn't talking to the cat.

I don't remember falling asleep, but I must have, because the next thing I knew, it was late afternoon. The darkness shattered, flinging me mercilessly back into reality. I jerked upright with a gasp. I frantically scanned the room and tried to figure out who or what had woken me, but there was nothing there except for my cat, who was quietly cleaning himself on the end of the bed.

I groaned and stood up. I wasn't about to try going back to sleep. If anything, I felt worse than before. My head was throbbing, and my wrists were red and sore. But most disconcerting was the fact that my face was still tender. I stared at my cheek in the wardrobe mirror and tried to decide if it looked swollen. Wincing, I laid my hand on my face and desperately prayed that it wouldn't bruise.

I changed back into my t-shirt and ripped jeans, which Mrs. Tang had washed. Shrugging on my leather jacket, I grabbed my backpack and made sure Nic's phone and the tablet the Tangs had loaned me were inside. I slid on a pair of house shoes out of respect for the family but grabbed my walking boots, intending to put them on as soon as I got downstairs. I had to get out of this house.

Tommy darted past me as I opened the bedroom door and disappeared down the stairs. I ran to follow him and nearly tripped over Nic. He sat on the top step, elbows propped on his knees, watching the stairwell in silence.

He looked up at me and frowned. "You're up already?"

I shrugged. "How long have you been sitting there?"

"Not long enough," he returned. "The doctor said he gave you some sleep medication—you should have slept at least six hours."

I rubbed my temple. At least that explained why my head hurt and the world was fuzzy around the edges.

Nic stood up as if to block the stairs. "You need to go lie back down."

I cringed; I wasn't nearly medicated enough to want to go back in that room. "I'm not tired," I lied.

He glared at me, but I shot him a look that begged him not to push it. He relented and stepped aside. "Then we may as well get this over with. Jael is ready to see you."

Lanzhou and Bowen met us downstairs. We took a short motorbike ride back to the factory, where they led us up to a conference room on the second level. The room looked like it belonged in a different century than the rest of the building. A wall of one-way mirrored windows flooded the room with brilliant afternoon sunlight, while a glowing digital whiteboard covered the opposing wall. Behind the head of the conference table, a terminal in the ceiling projected a 3D rending of meeting notes like a hologram.

I would have been fascinated by it had the bright lights not worsened the pounding in my head. I turned away from the windows and scanned the faces in the room. A dozen people were gathered around the sleek metal table, at the head of which resided Jael.

At least, I presumed it was Jael by the way she commanded the room. Her pull on the crowd was magnetic, as if she had redistributed gravity around her. She wasn't particularly tall, but she didn't need to be: Her giant turban and bright green heels added eight inches. She wore a sharp black skirt set that was contrasted with layers of colorful jewelry. She sat with one leg crossed smartly over the other as she listened with an air of motherly benevolence to the talk around the table.

Everyone silenced when we entered. Jael rose and beckoned to me. "Philadelphia." Her accent embellished the name into a title that sounded far too regal for me. "What an honor to finally meet you."

I took the invitation and walked up to her. After a moment of internal debate, I offered my hand.

She glanced at it and clicked her tongue. "No offense but… you haven't had your chip removed, have you?"

I flushed and shook my head.

She smiled reassuringly. "May I?"

I held my right hand out. She gently grabbed it and flipped it over, careful not to touch my palm. She pulled a small device out of her skirt pocket. It was slender like an old phone, its screen cluttered with unreadable code. She slowly passed it over my palm, murmuring with interest.

"This is going to make me sound like a geek…" She chuckled and put the device back in her pocket. "But that's some fascinating programming. A genius device, really."

I managed a smile. That sounded like something my brother would say.

She let go of my hand to gesture at the empty chairs next to hers. "We'll make arrangements to get that removed as soon as we're done here. But please, have a seat. We have much to discuss."

I took the seat to her right. John and Dowe waved at me from across the table, mouthing "hi" like we were mischievous schoolkids. Nic quickly claimed the spot next to me. Lanzhou sat on his other side and dropped the key to his motorbike on the table.

Jael settled back on her throne and fixed Nic with a reprimanding glare. "Q, were weapons necessary for this meeting?"

I threw a glance at Nic. *How did she…?*

Nic grunted and unzipped his jacket. He yanked his gun from its holster, switched it off, and threw it on the table in front of him. Several people murmured around the room.

I stared at the weapon as the light faded from the buttons. He'd had the weapon warmed up and ready to fire. He still didn't trust Jael—and after what happened last night, I didn't blame him.

"Thank you. Before we begin, Philadelphia…" Jael drew my attention back to her. "Please accept my sincere apologies, and those of the Tangs, for last night's incident. They assure me that the guard responsible and his associates have been dealt with."

I glanced down at Lanzhou, who dipped his head in an apologetic bow.

I swallowed. If only an apology could wipe the feeling of being violated from my nerves. "And what about Jayde?" I dared to ask.

"That depends on how quickly he returns my calls," she replied, the threat unveiled in her tone. "But rest assured that I'm keeping a very close eye on his internet activity. If he—or anyone I don't trust—checks in anywhere nearby, my people will get there first." She leaned across the table and laid her hand gently over mine. "I promise, he will not hurt you."

I stared down at her brightly colored nails, not sure I believed her. No one else had been able to protect me from Jayde; what made her think she could?

She withdrew her hand. "We'll see how Jayde responds, but I'm aiming to keep this debacle between us. I have a feeling he'll be more cooperative once he finds out I'm involved."

"And how are you involved in this?" Nic demanded.

"And who are you exactly?" I added, which seemed the more important question.

She grinned at us both. "I'm what you would call a tech mogul. I own one of the largest internet service providers in the world—which is also, incidentally, how I'm involved in this."

She stroked her fingers across the tablet inlaid in the conference table. The projection behind her chair went blank, then snapped back into focus. There, in full color, was an eerily 3D rendering of a video I wished I could forget: the security footage from Rott.

I flinched. I was already struggling to keep the memories of last night at bay; I didn't need to be assaulted with more horrors from my past. Thankfully, the sound on the video was muted. I deliberately turned away, focusing instead on the flashing bangles on Jael's wrists. They clacked together as she narrated with her hands.

"We were aware that the government was developing something on Rott, so I sent my agents to investigate."

"She means us!" John and Dowe squealed, and then gave each other a high-five.

I winced as the sharp sound made my ears ring. "You guys are… spies?"

Dowe folded his arms and dropped his voice an octave. "The name's Dowe. John Dowe."

"Please don't *ever* do that again," Nic groaned.

"I just… would have never guessed you guys were spies," I managed. *Or were employed at all.*

"Exactly," Jael beamed. "They're some of my best."

"So glad she assigned the pick of the litter to our case," Nic muttered, quietly enough that probably only I heard. I would have found it funny if my head wasn't spinning. I was in no frame of mind to process information this outlandish. Maybe Nic was right; maybe I should have gone back to bed.

Jael swiveled her chair to face the projection. "We discovered that the United was planning to mass produce a weapon, but they hadn't secured the formula yet. When they sent Ambrose to retrieve Dr. Nic, I knew we had to get him out of there."

I turned to Nic, who looked equally surprised by this revelation. "You were going to rescue me?" he scoffed, incredulous and ungrateful.

"We *tried* to rescue you, bro," Dowe insisted.

"You were supposed to order pizza!" John thumped his hands on the table.

Nic copied the gesture, making my headache even worse. "I didn't know! That coupon didn't exactly come with redemption instructions."

John cocked his head to the side. "Yeah, it did. It's in the fine print on the back."

"Enough," Jael mercifully interrupted. "What's done is done. Unfortunately, the United got the formula before I could intervene, and Thames sent you two back to Rott. And then this happened."

I saw a flash of colors out of the corner of my eye and instinctively turned to look at the projection. It was the moment everything changed: the moment I came on screen and identified myself to the world.

Jael grinned and spread her hands. "Our Blue Fire was born."

Something about her choice of words sent a weight dropping into my stomach, like someone had cut the line on an elevator. "I don't... I don't understand."

She rotated her chair back to face me. "I was watching the whole time. As soon as I saw this clip, I knew I'd found my thunderbird."

Her statement slammed into my heart, shattering my reality on impact. Nic's words came rushing back to me like a gust of cold air.

God didn't choose you for anything, Phil.

"To be fair," Jael typed on the tablet as she continued to explain, "the 'Blue Fire' imagery was Jayde's idea. He leaked the video before I was ready, but no harm done. The association served us well."

"No harm done?" Nic screeched. "You and I must have very different definitions of that word."

Jael misinterpreted his comment. "I had been planning to release the video myself, but I was hoping to extract you two first. I sent Tower the order to have you deported to the mainland, where my team was going to intercept you."

"My uncle knew?" I asked, even though I couldn't remember formulating the question. My voice sounded faint and echoey to my own ears, like it belonged to someone else. Like *I* belonged to someone else.

Jael nodded. "Unfortunately, after you arrived on the mainland, Thames got to you first. We didn't know Nolan was involved at the time, so I had no way of tracking where he'd taken you. While we were searching for you, Jayde leaked your first video. So I seized the opportunity and made it trend."

Her statement cycled around and around in my head like a warning siren. "You're the reason I trended," I whispered, afraid that if I spoke louder, it would make it true.

Jael grinned, revealing a row of perfect teeth. "I made you, Blue Fire."

I sank back in the chair and grabbed the seat—first with one hand, then the other. I gripped the plastic, desperate for something solid as everything I thought I knew crumbled away.

Nic was right. God hadn't chosen me. Jael had.

"How'd you manage that without getting arrested?" Nic demanded. He furrowed his brow, like this whole situation was a math problem to be solved. "Surely the government can review the analytics and figure out it was you who let it slip through the algorithm."

Jael's eyes sparkled, as if she'd been waiting all day for someone to ask. "As an internet service provider, I control the algorithm in my region. One of my biggest markets is Africa, which the West still considers to be 'third world.'"

She tapped the tablet, and a complicated pie chart appeared on the projector. "Being labeled as 'underdeveloped' has its perks. With the exception of a few population centers, the United doesn't care what most of the two billion people on my continent are doing. They're too busy negotiating for cobalt to keep their precious electric cars on the road. Besides, Africa has always been behind the world average in internet accessibility—who's going to know if I don't report a couple thousand users here and there?"

She smirked coyly, as if she'd just unlocked the key to the universe. I looked at Nic to see if this was making any sense to him. He was studying the chart on the screen, eyes flicking as he scanned the text.

"For the first forty-eight hours, I released the video in select markets, focusing on areas with big populations and minimal government oversight," Jael continued to explain. "I let the keywords trend briefly in different regions, always changing the parameters so it would look like I was doing my job."

The diamond on her finger danced as she rapidly swiped through menus. The image on the projector cycled through analytics and graphs and statistics that must have meant something to her. All I could think was that each number, equation, and data point was breaking down my identity, reducing Blue Fire to a search term a single woman could control.

Blue Fire wasn't a miracle. She was a lie.

"We did the same thing in Russia, South America, rural China—anywhere United control isn't as strict. By the time we released the video to the wider market, the movement was already too big to contain. The internet did the rest—with some help from my friends in social media, of course," Jael finished with a grand sweep of her hands.

Nic let out his breath, low and threatening. "You have no idea what you've done."

"I created a freedom movement," she snapped. "*We* created a freedom movement. Philadelphia was the perfect candidate. An unscripted act of rebellion from the person you'd least expect, plus an explosive story about a secret government weapon—it was the ideal combination to drive views. I couldn't have created a better story myself."

"But you did create me," I said, my doubt forming into words. "This is all scripted."

Jael's giant earrings bounced as she tipped her head to the side and smiled at me. "Nothing about your defiance is scripted, honey. That's why you're the perfect thunderbird."

No, I wasn't. I wasn't the thunderbird—I wasn't anything. This was all an illusion. Everything about the Blue Fire movement had been manufactured by a human. I was nothing more than a product of the algorithm and creative editing, all curated for one woman's gain.

I choked as the realization filled my lungs like water. Jael was using me; she'd been using me this whole time. Everything that had happened to me over the last few months, all the lucky circumstances I thought were miracles, had been orchestrated by her or Asia. I had merely been a pawn in their game as they'd used my image to fight for power.

And I was so naïve that I believed *God* had called me. God didn't choose me; He didn't have anything to do with this. He didn't speak to me. I made it all up in my head. I let Jayde or the Devil or *someone* lie to me about how important I was, and in my pride, I thought I could save the world. I'd fed into the machine, and now hundreds of thousands of people were prepared to fight and die in a war I'd created.

Nic was right. I was not a hero.

And I was not going to let anyone use me ever again.

19: NIC

Well, that explains a lot.

I stared at the graph on the projection as my brain adopted this information into the equation. I found it strangely comforting to know that all the terrible and annoying things that had happened to us over the past few months weren't freak accidents. Even John and Dowe—I was relieved to learn that they had a function on this planet other than building my character.

Jael was a problem, however. She had almost as much intel on us as Asia did, and I doubted she would be happy when I announced Phil's retirement. She created Blue Fire; she wouldn't let her go without a fight. And given how much influence this woman had over the algorithm, I wasn't sure I wanted her to know about our new files, anyway.

Before I could rationalize that problem, however, Phil presented me with a bigger one. She gripped the edge of the table and shoved her chair back. "I am not your thunderbird," she snapped.

There were whispers around the table. I seconded her statement, but now was a terrible time to announce it. "Phil..." I warned.

Bowen tried to help. "Blue Fire—" he said, rising.

"I am not Blue Fire!" she screamed. She slammed her fist on the table, causing the tablet to rock and the projection to glitch.

Jael just arched an eyebrow. "Philadelphia. You need to calm down."

"Don't tell me to calm down!" She turned on her. "You've been using me! You're no better than Asia."

Jael, to her credit, didn't deny it. "It was necessary."

Poor choice of words.

Phil took a step back. "Funny," she retorted in a voice devoid of feeling, "that's exactly what Thames said to me."

Jael studied her, calculating. "You chose this, Philadelphia. You didn't have to record more videos. You know how important this is."

"Yeah, well, I was wrong." Phil's voice cracked, and for a flicker of a moment, she was a scared little girl again.

And then that girl died.

Phil took a deep breath through her nose and straightened. Her eyes glinted, the pain vanishing from her expression like a lake freezing over. She lifted her chin and declared to the entire room, "I'm not going to do it."

Lanzhou scraped his chair back. "Please, let's talk about this."

"Yes, let's. *In private,*" I added, reaching for her shoulder.

She shrugged me off. "There's nothing to discuss. I'm done. Nic and I are getting new files and going back to Mars."

If only it were that easy, but I could tell by the shift in the room that it wouldn't be. Bowen and Lanzhou shared a nervous glance. The guard near the door reached for his taser, even though he was too far away to have a clean shot. No one spoke.

Jael shifted in her chair. She had one final moment to regain control of the situation, one final opportunity to win back Phil's trust.

She didn't take it. She beckoned at the guard. "I'm afraid that won't be possible, Philadelphia."

Wrong answer.

Phil reacted before the guard could. She lunged and grabbed my gun off the table. Flicking it on, she planted her feet apart and aimed it at Jael.

"Then make it possible," Phil spat.

Someone gasped. It took a second to realize it was me.

"Drop your weapon!" someone behind me yelled.

Jael lifted a finger to stop him, and wisely so. I could tell by the stance of Phil's body that she was prepared to shoot—and she would not miss.

"Let us go," Phil demanded, "or I'll shoot."

Jael barely flinched. "I see we're still upset over the events of the past few days," she said, putting her feet on the floor and slowly raising her hands. "Perhaps we should have this conversation later—"

Phil apparently agreed whole-heartedly, because she shot her. It was a clean shot, too—straight to the heart. Jael slumped over instantly, her immaculate suit marred with a smoking scorch mark.

The room erupted in shouts. I stumbled back, tripping over my chair. "Philadelphia!"

"Don't worry, it was set on stun." She whipped around to face Lanzhou and aimed the gun at his face. "Keys," she demanded.

The guard in the corner of the room leveled his rifle, but I put my hand out. "You might reconsider. Jayde's the one who taught her how to shoot."

Lanzhou factored that into his calculations. "Stand down," he ordered after a breathless minute.

No one obeyed him. "I said stand down!" he shouted again.

The guard lowered his rifle. Everyone else gingerly eased back into their seats. Lanzhou waited until they had stopped moving before turning to Phil. "Consider what you're doing."

"I know exactly what I'm doing," she snapped, and I believed her. "Keys."

Lanzhou hesitated a moment more, then grabbed his motorbike key off the table and tossed it at me.

"We're leaving," Phil announced, as if there was any doubt. "And don't even think about following us. If you give me any trouble, I swear I will go online and tell the government exactly where to look."

The silence rang in the room. I stared at her as she filled me with an emotion she had never before inspired.

Fear.

Satisfied no one was going to make a move, Phil lowered the gun slightly but kept her finger on the trigger. "Let's go," she said to me.

"I don't think we have much of a choice at this point." I ran out into the hall, keeping a wary eye on the guard.

Phil backed out after me. She made one last threatening sweep with her weapon, then punched the button to close the door. "This way!" She held the gun out of sight underneath her jacket and took off running.

I struggled to keep up. She ran to the stairwell, wisely bypassing the elevator. We pounded down the stairs to the docks. She took the steps two at a time and managed to keep ahead of me.

Thankfully for all involved, there was no one in the employee lot where the bikes were parked. Phil ran up to Lanzhou's bike. "Drive," she ordered.

"Gun first," I returned, then realized that was a foolish way to talk to someone with a loaded weapon.

Mercifully, I was still on her whitelist. She powered off the weapon and tossed it at me. I holstered it and jumped on the bike. Phil climbed on behind me. I tensed as her sharp fingernails gripped my jacket.

I started the bike and peeled out of the parking lot. Thankfully, the gates were open for shift change, so I blew past security, scattering a few disgruntled workers. I turned onto a side street and revved the engine as much as it would go—which unfortunately wasn't much. I didn't trust the guards to heed Phil's warning, so I wanted to get us as far away from the factory as possible before Jael came to. Then we would hide out until everyone calmed down. I could only hope Phil would be more reasonable after the sleep medication fully wore off.

She, however, had her own plans. "Head for the bus station!"

"Why?" I shouted back over the grind of the engine.

"We need to get to the subway!"

"It's almost rush hour. There will be a huge wait for the bus."

"Then we'll walk. Turn here!" She leaned forward and pointed with her arm.

I decided I'd better not argue with her while we were both balanced on a bike I only sort of knew how to drive. I followed her haphazard directions as we wove through the neighborhood, twisting and turning across alleys to avoid the increasing traffic. Soon the roads grew too clogged, and Phil ordered me to brake and abandon the bike behind a dumpster.

She jumped off and ran almost before I came to a complete stop. I parked the vehicle and hid the key in the basket on the back, muttering an apology to Lanzhou. Then I took off after Phil.

"Wait!" I shouted.

"Keep up!" she unhelpfully yelled back.

She was too far away for me to physically stop her. I pushed myself to catch up as she darted down the street. She shoved through the afternoon crowd, ignoring the protests and shouts in Mandarin. I almost lost sight of her as she sprinted across the street without looking. A car screeched to a stop, barely missing her.

Thankfully, I could see where she was headed; the subway station was in the square across the street. I waited until the crosswalk was clear, then ran after her. "Phil! Philadelphia!"

She didn't turn. I broke past the last crowd and fairly screamed at her. "Phil, stop, please!"

It took her three more yards to slow down, like she was a speeding train trying to brake. "Don't yell my name in public places."

"That's the least of our concerns right now. Slow down."

"The subway entrance is just ahead," she returned, her back to me.

I finally caught up to her. "I'm aware, and it'll still be there if we catch our breath for a minute." I collapsed on a bench and hoped she would take the hint.

She relented, yanking her backpack off and tossing it on the bench next to me. She stomped a few paces ahead and stopped under a tree, glaring up at the leaves like they held all the answers.

After making sure she was distracted, I pulled her backpack closer and silently undid the zipper. As I'd hoped, the tablet she'd borrowed from the Tangs was in there. I turned it on and made sure it was online.

Phil didn't notice. "Are you ready to go?"

I zipped the backpack shut. "That depends on where we're going. You seem to have a plan—care to enlighten me?"

"Same thing we were always going to do: Get out of the city and call Ephesus. I thought that was your great idea all along."

I could tell fatigue was catching up to her, and her attempt at being bratty just came out sounding pathetic. I knew this was my window to get through to her.

I took a breath to filter the sarcasm from my voice. "Philadelphia, we need to talk."

"What's there to talk about?"

"The fact that you just shot someone and stole a bike, for starters. Please, sit down."

She didn't. "Don't you get it? You were right all along."

As much as I loved to be right, something about her tone told me that, maybe this time, I would rather be wrong.

"You were right about everything," she continued. She wrapped her arms around her chest, like that could keep the dark emotions inside. "God didn't choose me. He had nothing to do with this. I let my fame go to my head, and I made this whole thing up. I am not a hero."

I stared at her. I had, in fact, said that.

She roared and yanked on her short hair. "I am such an idiot! I can't believe I went through all of this for nothing."

"What do you mean?" I said slowly, realizing she was balancing on the precipice of something very dangerous.

She flicked her hand broadly, as if her life story were mere scribbles to be wiped off a whiteboard. "My dad, Rott, this *stupid* operation… I literally just got drugged and locked in a dark room for twelve hours, and for *what*?"

Her voice reached a pitch and shattered, drawing glances from passersby. I stared at the red welt on her cheek as the events of recent months flashed through my mind. This fragile teenage girl had been through immeasurable trauma, and she hadn't gotten a moment's rest. She hadn't received any therapy, and she'd been forced to make terrible decisions no child should even have to consider. All the adults in her life had failed her.

Including me.

She laughed, a sinister, unhinged sound. "Do you know why I did it?"

I swallowed, but she didn't wait for me to gather my wits. "I did it because I thought God wanted me to. I really thought He'd called me. I really thought I'd heard from Him."

Her voice stretched into a plead, as if she was begging someone, anyone to believe her. I knew she was telling the truth. I knew that's exactly why she did it, and that was the only thing that had kept her from having a mental breakdown before now. Her faith in God was the only thread that had prevented her from becoming the villain of her own story.

And I'd broken that thread.

"I really thought this was the 'right thing to do.'" She mocked her own existence with air quotes. "But it wasn't."

Yes, it was, that voice in my head reminded me. And, for the first time in a long time, I agreed with Him.

"Phil—" I started.

She wasn't listening. "They all lied to me!" She yanked the jade bangle off her wrist and hurled it at the ground. I flinched—but thankfully, she missed. The bracelet clipped the edge of the sidewalk and bounced harmlessly into the dirt.

Phil gave an annoyed gurgle, as if she was frustrated with her inability to complete this simple task. "Come on," she snapped. She grabbed her backpack and strode towards the subway entrance.

I scooped up the bangle and jogged after her. We passed the defunct ticket scanners and started down the stairs to the platform. It was the beginning of rush hour, and the queue snaked halfway up the stairwell already. We joined the back of the line. Phil stared straight ahead, her back to me.

I looked down at the bangle in my hand. She'd chipped it on the concrete. I fingered the rough edge, remembering all the coffee cups, beakers, and soup bowls I'd sacrificed to my anger. I remembered the moment I'd hurled the contents of an entire table onto the floor, reeling from Asia's betrayal. That was the moment I'd determined to finish Red Rain. That was the moment I'd told the voice in my head to shut up and decided to do things my way.

And I realized, if I didn't pull Philadelphia back from the brink, she was going to end up exactly like me.

"Phil," I said, nudging her arm.

"What?" she snapped without looking back.

I glanced around. The old man in front of us was so ancient that he probably couldn't hear even if we shouted, and the teens who had joined the line behind us all had headphones. I took a deep breath and turned to face Philadelphia.

"They didn't lie to you."

"What do you mean?" Her voice was short, almost like she didn't care about the answer.

"They didn't lie to you," I repeated, making sure I was heard. "I did."

For the first time since we'd left the warehouse, she turned and looked up at me.

I met her gaze. "I lied to you. He does want you to do this." I omitted proper names in case there were any eavesdroppers.

She snorted. "You're just saying that to make me feel better." She looked away again.

"No, I'm not." I grabbed her shoulder and tried to turn her back towards me. "I've seen it. The Nolans, the party invite, everything—He wants you here."

She furrowed her brow. "What do you mean you *saw* it?"

I hesitated. My inclination was my best kept secret, but if she was going to believe me, she had to have the whole truth.

"I mean I *saw* it. The night before last, when you claimed you were never supposed to be a Nolan—I saw it all. You, in Beijing, as a Nolan, on even playing ground with Asia. He showed me."

She frowned at me like I was insane—which was how most normal people reacted when I told them I had an open vision. "You don't really believe that."

The line surged forward as a train pulled into the station, relieving the platform of a couple hundred people. Phil shrugged out of my grasp and ran down the steps.

I caught up with her. "You think I'd make something like *that* up? Trust me, I've tried to return this gift to sender several times."

"Stop patronizing me, Nic," she groaned. "I know what you really believe."

What do I really believe?

The line shuffled forward again. Phil squeezed a step ahead, putting the old man between us.

I knew I was losing her. She was no fool, and I'd spent too many days breaking down this bridge to lie my way across it. There was no amount of charismatic speaking that could convince her to go through with this if my heart wasn't in it. I had to decide right here, right now, what I believed, or I was taking her to hell with me.

I traded places with the old man, apologizing in Mandarin as I shoved him up a step. I stood next to Phil and spoke just loud enough for her to hear.

"I believe in God."

I took a deep breath as those words erased a thousand sins.

Phil was less forgiving. "That's great," she mocked. "Even the demons believe, and at least it makes *them* tremble."

"Yeah, and why do you think I ran the other way?" We shuffled forward a few more steps, and I leaned over and tried to get in her line of vision. "You want to talk about faith by actions—why do you think I've been trying to get us to go back to Mars? Because I know what you're supposed to do, and I know that if you stay in Beijing... then that means I have to stay too."

She jerked, as if my words had finally pierced through her armor. I saw the anger in her expression crack, and when she spoke again, I heard her: the old Philadelphia. "You—you mean that? But you said—"

"I know what I said," I cut her off, but gently. "Phil, I said those things because I didn't want to go back. I don't want to stay here and play politics. Don't you think I've seen this all before?"

Unbidden, the memories of my idealistic younger self reared their foolish head, and I remembered all the reasons why I'd lied to her in the first place. I twisted the bangle in my fingers and sighed. "You're in the exact same position I was when I met Asia. I had money, influence, and political connections. I could have done something. But after what she did to my parents..."

I didn't have to finish the sentence. As the words left my mouth, I finally understood why God had chosen Philadelphia.

It wasn't because she was anyone special. It wasn't because she had done anything particularly amazing. It wasn't even because she was in the right place at the right time.

He had chosen her because she had said *yes*—when I had said *no*.

I remembered the moment I'd taken my life back into my own hands. I'd walked to the whiteboard, the one covered with the incomplete formula for Red Rain, and told God I was going to do it myself. The way I saw it, doing things God's way had cost me my parents' lives. If that was how the game was played, I might as well do it my way and save myself in the process.

I am no better than they are.

I'd said no to God that day—and then time and time again, I'd refused His counteroffers. I could have taken responsibility for my crimes instead of using Smyrna as my scapegoat, forcing him to complete the formula. I could have helped Philadelphia destroy the factory instead of trying to salvage Red Rain, nearly killing her in the process. I could have helped her find her father instead of letting her go back to Earth alone. I could have helped her be the leader she was called to be—instead of letting her fight a war by herself and then yelling at her when she made stupid choices.

I'd said no to God's call on my life. But now, standing next to me—looking up at me with vulnerable, bloodshot eyes—was one final offer.

We reached the platform. I glanced up and realized there was only a short line between us and the subway. If we squeezed, we could make it on the next train. It was now or never—and if I thought about it too hard, *never* still looked very tempting.

I took a breath and turned to face her. "Look, I still don't want to stay here, and I don't expect that to change any time soon. But I know what I saw. I know what you're supposed to do, and I know you need my help. So, I'm making the decision to do what you've always done." I held the bangle out to her.

She took it very slowly. "And that is?"

"Do it anyway."

I scanned the platform and spotted a gap in the crowd that led to the exit—back to Beijing, Jael, the revolution. I turned to look at Philadelphia where she stood behind me on my left. She watched me, waiting.

I smiled and held out my left hand.

20: PHILADELPHIA

What have I done?

I stared at the bangle in my hand. The feel of the cold jade brought reality crashing back down on me, and I wasn't sure I liked what I remembered.

Did I really shoot someone? What if she's hurt? Oh God, please let her be okay! What was I thinking, running away? I can't believe I stole Lanzhou's bike! How am I going to fix this? I can't go back there and face them! They'll never forgive me! Oh Jesus, who have I become?

But even as the shame and grief swirled around in my head like a dust storm, several other truths solidified out of the noise.

I knew I didn't make this up! I knew I heard from God. I know what God's voice sounds like.

I had the Holy Spirit. If I'd had any doubts about what God was saying, I should have tried the spirits and found the answer for myself. But instead, I'd let a bunch of humans—Nic, Jayde, Jael—reframe my truth. I'd let their words *and* my own fears convince me that God was lying to me.

And all the while, God had been showing Nic the same things, confirming His Word to both of us.

I stared at the back of Nic's head as he scanned the crowd. Had he really seen all that, about me? Why would God show him my future? What did any of this have to do with Nic?

Nic's last words echoed back to me. *"I know what you're supposed to do, and I know you need my help."*

I clenched my fist around the bangle as the last piece of the puzzle, the checkmate in the game of chess we'd been playing for the last nine months, snapped into place. This was why God had sent my family to Mars in the first place, why He'd allowed me to get tangled up in Wing 74 and Red Rain. It was because He knew I needed Dr. Nic Von Nieuwenhuyse.

If there was anyone who could help me fight Beijing politics and confront Asia, it was Nic.

Motion in my peripheral distracted me. I looked up to see Nic turning to me with the rarest of expressions: a smile.

And then he held out his left hand.

I stared at it, knowing full well it was an invitation to a life I didn't fully understand yet. But it was the life God called me to have—the life He called us *both* to have.

Nic arched an eyebrow and wiggled his fingers. "If you leave me hanging for too long, I will take it back. You know how I hate physical affection."

I grinned, a sliver of joy finding its way into my soul. Sliding the bangle back on my wrist, I reached out and grabbed Nic's hand with my right.

Our palms contacted—and I felt a shock. I must have built up static electricity in the stairwell.

Nic felt it too. He dropped my hand and jerked back, as if it had caused him a lot of pain. "What the—"

He never finished. He hesitated, for a split second looking panicked, and then he collapsed.

"Nic!" I screamed as his head hit the tile with a crack.

The displaced crowd grumbled and stumbled around us, and I feared he might be trampled. I shoved someone aside and dropped down next to his head. I shook his shoulder with both hands. "Nic! Get up!"

He didn't respond. And that's when I realized he wasn't breathing.

"Nic!" My terror turned the name into a bloodcurdling wail.

Oh God, oh God, help!

The murmur in the crowd changed pitch. "He's not breathing!" I yelled. "Someone help!"

Several people shouted. A man shoved his way through the crowd and knelt next to Nic. He held his fingers to Nic's neck, then immediately planted his hands on his chest and started pumping.

I watched in fascinated horror as he alternated between compressions and deep breaths into Nic's mouth and nose. He repeated the maneuver with relentless efficiency, pausing only to call to someone in the crowd. Time seemed to freeze over as the stranger tried desperately to pump life back into Nic's body.

Jesus, save him!

Nothing changed. I wasn't sure if ten seconds or ten minutes had passed, but I could tell the man was getting frustrated. He paused to check Nic's pulse again, then grunted and resumed compressions.

No, God, no!

A subway employee darted up to us and dropped an orange box on the floor. The other man unzipped Nic's jacket. There were some gasps over Nic's holstered gun, but the man ignored it and ripped Nic's shirt open. He pulled two wired patches off the box and arranged them on Nic's chest. Then he punched a button on the keypad.

The device beeped. Nic's body twitched, but his heart did not respond. The man tried again. Still no movement. I watched as Nic's face and neck began to turn purple.

No, God, don't do this! I need him!

A young woman pushed her way up to the subway employee. She held out her phone and asked a question. He shouted something in Mandarin into the receiver.

Someone behind me translated. "He said it's sudden cardiac arrest."

As soon as he said it, I knew what had happened. The chip in my palm.

I looked down at my right hand.

Nic was dying. And I killed him.

TO BE CONTINUED...

THERE'S MORE TO THE STORY…

I hated parties.

As a general rule, they involved too many people and too little productivity. State dinners were even worse, as the majority of the attendees had no business being there. The dregs of society tended to wash up at government events, floating in on the sponsorship of privileged friends. They would cling like mollusks to affluent attendees, muddying the waters for those of us who had actual work to accomplish.

That's the only reason I came to this particular government function. I had been presented with an award and was a keynote speaker, but the only thing I wanted to walk away with was more sponsors for my experiments.

On account of said award, I could have had anyone in the room I wanted, but most of them were not worth my time. Because of the sensitive nature of my work, I needed a very specific kind of patron.

Those in the upper echelons of society weren't worth the risk; they had everything to lose and nothing to gain. Those in the lower ranks didn't have the resources I needed. But the aspiring politicians in the middle—those were my primary targets. They had enough money to be useful to me, and they had everything to gain. An underappreciated director with a shot at a higher seat was willing to bend the rules if it meant winning valuable allies. If I found one who was disgruntled enough, they might even be willing to help me break the system entirely.

I spent the evening filtering the crowd, searching for the up-and-coming. I would introduce myself, allow them to flatter themselves a bit, and then sow a seed of hope—the mere suggestion that I could be useful to them. Then I would walk away, leaving them to simmer in their imagination for a while. By the time I returned, they were ready to sign.

It was a delicate process that involved balancing a dozen active leads simultaneously. I couldn't afford to get distracted—which was why I was extremely annoyed when the daughter of Chairman Mong approached me.

Anyone else would have been beside themselves. As third in line to the General Secretary, Chairman Mong had earned the privilege of not talking to people. Instead, he spied out his prey from across the room and sent one of his lesser councilmen to make the arrangements.

His daughter, a chairwoman of some standing in her own right, also had the honor of being his carrier pigeon. She spent the evening watching his face for subtle nods and gestures. I knew this because she and I had inadvertently exchanged several glances.

As she strode towards me, her clicking stilettos heralding her approach, I realized that those glances may have been intentional on her part.

I decided to cut her off at the pass in hopes of keeping the intrusion brief. I met her halfway across the ballroom and offered my hand. "Madame Mong, I'm Dr. Nic."

She clasped my hand with a fearless grip. "Shi Min Tai," she offered.

I blinked. She'd skipped at least three phases of formal introduction and jumped straight to given names.

Well, that escalated quickly.

"Charmed," I said, and lightly pumped her hand. "Which do you prefer?"

"Excuse me?"

"If we are going on a first name basis, three given names seems excessive. Which do you prefer?"

She grinned, showing perfect teeth. "The boys in Washington call me Asia." She withdrew her hand from mine, slowly, her fingers brushing my palm. "But I prefer Min."

I hesitated, fully aware of the risks associated with that invitation.

She waited patiently.

I accepted the offer. "Pleasure to meet you, Min." In exchange, I offered her one of my rare smiles—the most valuable currency I had on me at the moment.

She seemed pleased with the sacrifice. "Congratulations on the award. From what I've heard, you deserve it."

"You seem to think so."

My prophetic insight stumped her, as it did with everyone. She arched one thin, penciled eyebrow. "I'm sorry?"

"Forgive me for noticing, but your father didn't send you over here."

She instinctively glanced back at him. Chairman Mong hadn't paid me any mind all evening, for which I was grateful. I was not interested in bargaining with him; he was one of the people I hoped would suffer when I succeeded.

No, Min had sought me out of her own volition—a fact I found extremely suspicious.

When she turned back to me, her dark eyes glinted like stars swallowed by a black hole. "You're a smart man, Nic."

"I wouldn't be worth your time if I wasn't." I shifted and glanced around the room. Several jealous—and prying—eyes were angled in our direction, no doubt wondering what wizardry I had pulled to secure Min's attention. Whatever she wanted, she'd better make it fast.

I turned back to her and spread my hands. "What can I do for you, Min?"

She devoured my subservience with a ravenous grin. "I want to sponsor your project."

"I'd be honored," I said, even though I wasn't. I did not like people who volunteered their money without first listening to my speech. That meant they had something to gain—something I hadn't sold them. "May I ask what interests you about my work?"

She opened her diamond-encrusted clutch and rifled through the contents. "The science speaks for itself, doesn't it?"

Of course it did—but not to people like Min. My project was, by design, deceptively mundane. I had developed a unique blend of plastic that was resistant to almost every acidic compound on the spectrum. The result had significant implications for the medical and industrial fields, but that was hardly the kind of advancement that concerned people of Min's status.

She withdrew a lipstick from her purse. "I think the science has other... uses, don't you?"

It did. That was the whole reason I developed it—because I ultimately intended to store something other than cleaning products in the canisters.

And that was exactly why I had to be very careful about who got involved.

I pretended to straighten my bowtie. "Is the Chairman interested in other applications?"

"Hardly." With a deft hand, she swiped a fresh layer of bloodred paint on her lips. "But I might be."

"'Might'?" I fought the urge to laugh. "As much as I love a good experiment, that is not a probability I want to test."

She clicked her lipstick case shut. "Not a man to take a risk, are we, Dr. Nic?"

The insult tickled my rage, and I realized I'd lost the upper hand in the conversation a long time ago. "I am quite comfortable taking risks," I snapped. "But only necessary ones."

"As am I. I hate an unnecessary mess." She dropped the lipstick in her purse and looked up at me. "But I can assure you this is a well-calculated risk."

Clearly, she was now trying to sell me on the deal, so I deferred the stage to her. "What are your terms?"

"I have some personal projects you may be able to help me with in the future." She looked up and met my eyes. "But in the meantime, I've looked at your portfolio. I know people who can fund everything on your list. I would be happy to introduce you."

I filtered her words through my mental translation program, trying to decode any pauses or inflections that might tell me what she was up to. If I said yes, I'd be dancing with the devil; her father could ruin me with a finger snap.

But if she meant what she said, I could have everything I wanted—and a clear shot at her father when I was ready to take it.

I held out my hand. "I expect my project to cost a great deal of money."

She took it with a smile. "Leave it to me."

AVAILABLE NOW!

WANT EXCLUSIVE BONUS SCENES?

Become a Patron and get access to **exclusive bonus scenes** for this book! This bonus content is not available anywhere else, and I post a new scene every month. Plus, you can get digital ARCs, signed paperbacks, collector's edition hardbacks, and merch, or read my WIP as I write it!

Become a Patron at:
patreon.com/rachelnewhouse

Or sign up for my newsletter and be the first to hear about new releases—plus get sneak peeks of upcoming books, cover art, and more!

Sign up at:
rachelnewhouse.com/subscribe

DID YOU LOVE THIS BOOK?

Please consider leaving a review on Amazon or Goodreads! It's one of the most important things you can do to support an indie author. Thank you!

HI FROM RACHEL

Rachel Newhouse is an author, wife, secretary, and Sunday school teacher from Kansas City, Missouri. Her obsessions are sci-fi, dystopian, and kid lit. When she's not writing, she's cooking Asian food, growing chilis that are too spicy to eat, and watching wildly age-inappropriate shows like *My Little Pony* and *Gravity Falls* with her husband, Joe. She also really likes glitter. You've been warned.

Connect with Rachel:
bio.site/rachelnewhouse